The Game She Hates

An Opposites Attract Christian Romance

Ella Marie

Copyright © 2024 by Ella Marie – All rights reserved

In no way is it legal to reproduce, duplicate, or transmit any part of this document in either electronic means or in printed format. Recording of this publication is strictly prohibited and any storage of this document is not allowed unless with written permission from the publisher.

All rights reserved.

Scripture quotations are from the ESV®Bible (The Holy Bible, English Standard Version®), copyright© 2001 by Crossway Bibles, a publishing ministry of Good News Publishers. Used by permission. All rights reserved.

Scripture quotations taken from the (NASB®) New American Standard Bible®, Copyright © 1960, 1971, 1977, 1995, 2020 by The Lockman Foundation. Used by permission. All rights reserved.

Contents

Dedication	VI
Content Warnings	1
1. Zane Ortiz	2
2. Pearl Davis	7
3. Pearl Davis	13
4. Pearl Davis	21
5. Zane Ortiz	26
6. Zane Ortiz	31
7. Pearl Davis	37
8. Zane Ortiz	43
9. Pearl Davis	49
10. Zane Ortiz	56
11. Zane Ortiz	60
12. Pearl Davis	66

13.	Zane Ortiz	71
14.	Pearl Davis	79
15.	Zane Ortiz	85
16.	Pearl Davis	90
17.	Zane Ortiz	97
18.	Zane Ortiz	103
19.	Pearl Davis	107
20.	Zane Ortiz	115
21.	Pearl Davis	123
22.	Zane Ortiz	129
23.	Pearl Davis	137
24.	Zane Ortiz	146
25.	Pearl Davis	154
26.	Pearl Davis	162
27.	Zane Ortiz	167
28.	Pearl Davis	173
29.	Zane Ortiz	181
30.	Zane Ortiz	190
31.	Pearl Davis	197
32.	Zane Ortiz	205

33.	Pearl Davis	213
34.	Zane Ortiz	219
35.	Pearl Davis	229
36.	Epilogue	236
Thank you		241
Also by Ella Marie		243
About the author		244

"I do all things for the
sake of the gospel, so
that I may become a
fellow partaker of it."
1 Corinthians 9:23

For the girlies who cherish and long for the gift of Christ-centered relationships in both their love life and friendships.

Content Warnings

This is a heartwarming Christian romance, while there isn't much grit or sorrowful moments on page, I still want you to feel safe diving in. Serious topics like the death of a parent (past), parental neglect and abuse (past), and struggles with alcoholism (past) are referenced respectfully without graphic detail. Expect clean language, and any swoony moment was delicately crafted with a younger audience in mind, promising a wholesome and God-honoring experience for all.

1

Zane Ortiz

I stride through the corridors of the arena, my heart still racing from the game. I knew it was coming—that summoning from Coach. But even as I approach his office, I can't ignore the surge of adrenaline still coursing through my veins.

I inhale deeply, steeling myself for what awaits. Coach left the door slightly ajar, which lets me know he's ready for me.

Going in feels like charging headlong into a storm. I know full well that he isn't pleased with me—a sentiment I'm all too familiar with.

Once inside, I take a moment to absorb the well-worn surroundings of his office. The cluttered desk stands as a bastion of his domain, decked with a mishmash of hockey memorabilia and scattered paperwork.

A framed jersey hangs proudly on the wall, emblazoned with the emblem of the Boston Bruins. It's not just any jersey; it's his old jersey, worn during his time as part of the team. The fabric shows signs of wear. It serves as a reminder to the team of where dedication and passion can lead. Next to it, a row of Glaciers trophies gleams under the fluorescent lights.

The wall behind his desk is decorated with at least a dozen photos, capturing moments of unity and triumph. My favorite among them is one of us hoisting last year's trophy, our faces etched with jubilation as we celebrated reaching the finals.

Amidst the accolades, a whiteboard in the corner displays game schedules and strategies. I finally shift my gaze in his direction. There, I notice the anticipation in his eyes, as though he's been waiting for me to acknowledge his presence and meet his gaze.

"What gets into your mind when you're out there?" Coach's voice breaks the silence, straight and to the point.

He doesn't offer a seat, but after that game, I feel like I need one. So, I pull out a chair and sit in front of him. I rub my knuckles together, feeling the tension crackling in the air.

"You're gonna suspend me?" I ask casually, though the weight of the question is anything but light. It wouldn't be the first time he's suspended me mid-season, but I know Coach Kendrick doesn't want to revisit that disaster. We both have something to lose, and I'm prepared to sit here and convince him that I couldn't care less.

"I know you don't want to be suspended, Ortiz, and that's not what this is about."

I exhale in response, surprised that Coach is letting this one go. Usually, he'd start lecturing me about my anger management issues, but tonight he seems to be skipping the part where I let loose on those Thunderhawks losers.

"You know Tyler is retiring soon, and I think you'd make a good captain."

I raise my eyebrows at the mention of being captain. Despite my best efforts to avoid team gossip, rumors about me replacing Tyler somehow found their way to me. Still, it catches me off guard that Coach thinks I'd make a good captain. He's one of two people in the world who really know me, albeit against my will, and he understands that captaincy is about more than just being the most competitive guy on the team or having some great skills.

"Name one thing Tyler and I have in common." I challenge him, knowing full well that Tyler and I couldn't be more different. He's a few years older, and his maturity seems to double his age. He's retiring to live a slower-paced life and spend more time with his family. He's a people person, known for his kindness, always checking in on each one of us during off-season, and he's always talking about his relationship with Jesus—whatever that's supposed to mean. I try not to give him too much of my time because even though he's not a party animal like most of the team, he's still not relatable in any way.

Coach leans forward, not breaking eye contact. "I've realized one thing about you, Ortiz," he says, his index finger tapping his jaw. "You may put on a tough front, but deep down, I know there's a heart that loves the team just as much as Tyler does."

I scoff inwardly. Love and I don't exactly go hand in hand. I've loved no one, and nobody has loved me—except for one person who had no choice but to devote their life to convincing me otherwise. But on the ice, there's nothing I wouldn't do for all the guys on the team. Even Trent. The most annoying guy on the team. On ice, I always pass to him and set him up for great goals. But off the ice, I don't want to give Trent the satisfaction of a response to his condescending, bullying self. He reminds me too much of my dad.

"Interesting observation, Coach," I reply, my tone guarded. "But I don't do relationships like Tyler does. You know I barely hang out with them, and if we're being candid, I don't think they'd want me as their captain either. Maybe Carson. He comes close, and he never throws punches."

"Listen, Ortiz. I know what you've been through, and that's why I've been patient with you. But I also see who you really are, trauma and heartbreak aside. I need you to see the person I see both on and off the ice."

I've never quite understood what Coach sees in me besides my dedication to hockey. Why can't he grasp that the ice is where I let out all the pent-up frustration that's been with me since birth? From the moment he plucked me from my old team in Chicago, he's never stopped pushing me to be better. And while I know it's all well-intended, I can't shake the feeling that I've always fallen short in everyone's eyes. Someday, he'll see it too, but for now, his unwavering commitment to me is like an itch I can't quite scratch—uncomfortable, yet oddly endearing because not many people have tried to commit to me like this.

I splay my hands in question. "And how do you suggest I see the version of me you see?" I ask, genuinely interested in what he's about to say.

Coach's answer stuns me. "Counseling," he replies, dead serious.

I wave off the suggestion with a dismissive snort. "That's ridiculous. Been there, done that. Therapists just rake in cash to listen to people whine. And trust me when I say they never actually fix anything."

"I'm not talking about just any therapist. I know just the person, and although she doesn't usually take on adults, I really think she'd work well with you," Coach says, his lips curling into a smile.

"Oh, now I need a pediatric therapist?" I ask incredulously, running my hand down my face.

He wears a serious expression. "I think revisiting your childhood will do you good, and you need someone with a fresh perspective, someone who's not tied to sports like all the counselors you've had before."

I chew on my lip. There's no way he's seriously considering a pediatric therapist for me.

2

Pearl Davis

Robyn bursts into my room, practically shouting, "I'm out of toothpaste. Can I grab yours?"

With a sigh, I respond from my prone position on the bed, not bothering to tear my gaze away from the wall. "Yeah, you can grab mine."

The silence that follows prompts me to glance her way. She's giving me that look, the one that says she's expecting more from me. "Actually, I think I have a new one in the top cupboard," I add hastily, hoping to deflect her disapproval.

I ignore her pointed stare and roll onto my back and groan inwardly. An unwelcome conversation is coming and there is nothing I can do to stop it.

"I don't like this one bit, P," Robyn says, drawing back the curtains that have seen little sun in the last few weeks. "You've got to stop wallowing in your pain and come back to church."

I bury my face in the pillow, trying to shield myself from the unwelcome sunlight that feels all too contrary to my inner darkness. "I can't, Robs," I mumble softly through the fabric. "I'm just not ready to see them."

"It's not just about Duke and Kate anymore, P," she insists, her tone softening from harsh to understanding. "It's about you missing church. And me sitting by myself again, like I haven't done my part in convincing you to become my best friend and roommate."

Robyn and I crossed paths over five years ago at church, and let me tell you, she had a stern expression that could scare away a whole litter of puppies. While everyone mistook her quiet demeanor for unfriendliness, I saw through her stoic exterior. We clicked instantly; there's no doubt that our friendship was predestined. She became my rock during the chaos of pursuing my master's in clinical psychology, and I like to believe I nudged her out of her comfort zone, teaching her the fine art of small talk along the way.

I dramatically toss the pillow aside and fix my gaze on her pixie-like face framed by short honey-blond hair. She's my favorite person in the entire universe, and with sincerity, but also a touch of theatrics, I deliver my line. "You never convinced me. The moment I laid my eyes on you, I knew you belonged in my corner." Then, attempting to maintain a straight face, I add, "But I really just want to tune in to the livestream today."

She puts her palm over her chest. "Touching, but no. Honestly, I've run out of excuses for why you've missed the last three Sundays. People are starting to worry about you, and it feels like lying to everyone who cares about you."

"It's not a lie. I really don't feel well. My heart is hurting, and it has been for a month."

"Don't act so clever." She swats my forearm. "The way I see it, Duke loves our church, and he's here to stay. And he and Kate? They look serious. So whether you like it or not, you're going to have to face them eventually."

I wince. "That's not the pep talk I was hoping for. Why do bad things happen to good people?" I grumble, "I did all the legwork. I met him first. I roped him into our church. I even got him interested in volunteering with the youth. And then he spots Kate and tosses me aside like a worn-out rag."

"In his defense, he had no idea you had this huge crush on him," Robyn points out, her logic cutting through my emotional haze. "And Kate was completely oblivious too. I bet if she knew, she wouldn't have been batting her eyelashes at him. So, you can't really blame either of them."

"Okay Robs, whose side are you actually on?" I love Robyn so much, and I know she is usually right and always so logical. That's how her brain works—everything is a solvable mathematical equation. But my heart operates on a completely different frequency.

"I'm on the side of getting you back to church. I don't think a *mere mortal* should come between your relationship with Jesus." Easy for her to say. She's never had romantic feelings for anyone.

Mine and Duke's encounter at Randy's coffee shop a couple of months ago was straight out of a rom-com. We hit it off when our coffee orders got mixed up, then when I returned to my seat, he mustered the courage to ask if he could join me. With his dark brows, his perfectly styled hair, and even his choice of attire on a Saturday morning, he had me swooning.

I couldn't resist talking to him, despite my initial intentions to focus on my work. That's just who I am—I talk to people for a living—well, younger people. I found myself drawn to him, and he was so kind. He opened up about a nonprofit organization he was involved in, and in that moment, I had to thank the Lord for bringing such an incredible man into my life. It felt like a perfect meet-cute, and in my mind, we tied the knot when he mentioned that he had recently moved from Boston and was looking for a new church in Bedford.

Naturally, I did what any good Christian would do—I invited him to church. Of course, I wanted him to find a spiritual home, but deep down, I also hoped to see him there every Sunday. And when he finally joined us, he sat with Robyn and me in our favorite back row. I couldn't contain my excitement.

The second Sunday, he chose to sit in the front row. And that's where he definitely saw Kate, one of the singers on the worship team—a beautiful brunette with blue eyes and the most angelic voice. After church, I approached him, asked him to join us for Youth Night on Wednesday. There were again double motives at play, but who's counting? Duke arrived, dressed in the most relaxed clothes I'd ever seen him wear—a polo and chinos.

I made the stupid mistake of introducing him to everyone, including Kate. The moment her eyes met his, I saw the same spark that ignited between us at the coffee shop. Ignoring my intuition, I proceeded to lead the Bible study for the youth with Robyn's help and a few others. But despite my efforts, Kate and Duke became close. Every time they laughed together, it felt like a hot knife slicing through my heart. Their attraction to each other was undeniable, and there was no stopping it.

A few weeks ago, they announced their relationship on Youth Night, and I must commend myself for not collapsing right then and there because it felt like my entire world was crumbling. I had seen their relationship coming, but them making it official so soon caught me off guard. I wasn't ready for it. So, I made the decision to avoid them at all costs. I can't bear to see them all lovey-dovey together. I know my feelings are irrational, and I've been praying for the Lord to oust this jealousy from my heart, but so far, my prayers remain unanswered.

"If you don't come for yourself, at least do it for me. You know how flustered I get when the deacons start prying into my dating life. I don't have the heart to tell them that, at nearly thirty, I'm still not ready to settle down and start a family," Robyn pleads, and I can't help but laugh because it's so true. The mere thought of marriage sends her running in the opposite direction. She's fiercely committed to her career goals. She rejects anything and anyone that dares to distract her from her fast-track journey to VP of Finance.

"Ugh, you convinced me," I concede, rolling out of bed and heading for the shower. "Let me get ready."

I hear Robyn's gentle knock on my door. "Hey, just wanted to let you know that we're running a bit late. But it's okay if you still need a minute."

I chuckle appreciatively at her consideration. Despite her eagerness to get me back to church, she's giving me the space I need to make the decision for myself. She's probably afraid I'll retreat back to bed and declare I'm not going. "I'm almost done," I shout back to reassure her.

As I stand here, torn on what to wear, memories of when Duke first started attending church flood my mind. I always dressed in my Sunday best, hoping to catch his eye. Fit and flare dresses, colorful knee-length skirts paired with nice blouses, and heels to match his polished appearance became my new norm. But now, I want to dress for myself, not for him. I opt for neutral slacks and a cozy burnt-orange cardigan.

3

Pearl Davis

I breathe a sigh of relief when the pastor finally takes the stage and starts preaching. With everyone settled into their seats, including Robyn and me in our trusty back-row spot, I can feel a sense of normalcy returning.

One of the perks of belonging to a small church is the familiarity and ease of conversation with just about everyone. But I'd rather be invisible today. I could see the worry etched on people's faces as they asked how I was doing. Rumors about my supposed appendix removal spread like wildfire, adding a bizarre twist to my heartbreak. I wonder if any of this was Robyn's fault. She had received so many questions about me and might have let people think the worst had happened.

From my vantage point, I spot Duke in the front row, his hair slicked back with what must be a gallon of hair gel, and his arm draped casually around Kate. That familiar pang of jealousy rears its ugly head once more. How is it that I still feel like I should be the one by his side, not her?

I barely know the guy beyond our initial coffee shop chat, when I let my imagination run wild with visions of our future together.

Robyn catches my gaze and nudges me in the ribs with her elbow. "Stop ogling them like that," she whispers. And she's right. I'm completely distracted, and that's not why I'm here.

As the pastor concludes his sermon, he invites anyone with prayer requests to come forward. It's a quaint tradition, where we pray for various needs, usually revolving around sickness or financial struggles. Nobody ever comes forward asking for prayers because their heart is broken, pleading for divine intervention after a member of the worship team stole the man they fancied. No, that scenario only happens in my melodramatic mind.

After a few prayer requests, to my utter shock, Kate and Duke stand up and grab the mic. I'm casually sipping water, minding my own business, when Kate drops the bombshell. "Duke and I got engaged yesterday. We'd love prayers and help planning our wedding. Since neither of us has family here, we want to include everyone in this church family on our journey."

I nearly spit out my water in disbelief. Engaged? Robyn wraps her arms around me, sensing my distress. I'm starting to hyperventilate. Something is seriously off. The room starts spinning, and I'm suddenly feeling queasy. Maybe I do need some prayers too because what exactly does she mean by *engaged*?

"Take deep breaths, P. It's going to be okay," Robyn reassures me.

"No, it's not okay. They met two months ago. How can they be engaged now?" I blurt out, my mind racing.

"Don't look at me. You're the hopeless romantic here," she shakes her head.

"But how is this possible? Did you have any clue about this? Is that why you insisted on me coming today?" I ask, desperation creeping into my voice.

"I would never do that to you. Plus you're closer to Kate than I am, and if you had no idea, you can bet I wasn't in the know either."

It's true; I've been keeping up the friendships for both of us. But now, could Kate and I even remain friends after this? It's unfair to her how I can't help but resent her for liking the same guy I did and winning him over. Nothing is her fault, but jealousy has been a disease that's made my life all too hard and far too complicated.

When we make our way out of the church, I steer Robyn toward the nursery side, eager to avoid any congratulatory encounters with Kate and Duke.

"Let's slip out through the nursery side. I can't handle pretending to be happy for them right now," I say, tugging at Robyn's arm. But as always after church, I see her scanning the parking lot. She's definitely checking to see if Kendrick came to church today. Like everyone in this town, Robyn is an avid hockey fan and the coach of her favorite team is a close friend of mine. He also happens to attend our church. I squeeze her arm tightly. "No, Robyn, not this time. Please, we have to go."

"But, P, just imagine the seat he's gonna hook me up with for next week's game. Please?"

"I'll give you his number, and Kendrick can sort you out next week," I promise, exasperated. "Just not here, okay?"

"I'm begging you P. I just saw his Mercedes-Benz S-Class. And you know he simply adores you. If I ask him and we're together, he has no choice but to give me a free ticket," she pouts.

I roll my eyes. I don't understand people and their addiction to sports. Robyn is the weirdest of them all. She'll go to a game, have the time of her life, and then come back home to watch a replay of that same game. If I were a sports junkie, hockey would be the last sport I'd want to watch. It looks so scary to me—people skating and slamming into each other for a living.

Before I can change her mind, I hear Kendrick's voice behind us. "Pearl Davis. Just the girl I wanted to see." I turn to meet his tall, sturdy frame, his broad shoulders hinting at years of athleticism. Despite his age, which is only apparent in his salt-and-pepper hair, he carries himself with vigor. Behind wire-rimmed glasses, his warm hazel eyes shine with kindness. He's dressed in a navy jacket over a crisp button-down shirt.

I catch Robyn's wide grin in my peripheral vision. "Hi, Kendrick, how is Gabe?" I ask, realizing it's been a while since I checked in on his son. He adopted Gabe from the child foster care system, and I had the privilege of working with Gabe for six months as his therapist. Despite the progress he made, Kendrick's tone leaves me concerned—perhaps there's been a setback in Gabe's mental health.

"Gabe is fantastic," Kendrick responds with a proud smile. "He's become such a great communicator, and Lisa and I only have you to thank."

I offer a shy smile. "No need. He's a great kid who just needed the right support. I'm glad he found you."

"You're always so sweet, Pearl," Kendrick remarks. "But I wanted to ask you something, more like a favor than anything."

"Anything for you, Kendrick," I reply without hesitation.

"Remember you said that in a minute," he says, glancing around to ensure privacy. Robyn takes a tiny step back, respecting his unspoken request. "So I have this guy on my team. He's carrying a lot of childhood baggage that's holding him back. He's closed off and refuses to let anyone in. Maybe you could work with him?"

I realize I might have misjudged Kendrick's request. "I'm sorry, Kendrick. I'm strictly on the pediatric side of things. I don't work with adults, and definitely not athletes. But I promise to find a counselor for him."

He adjusts his glasses and leans in closer to me, as if about to share a secret. But, his years of coaching haven't honed his whispering skills. "Ortiz doesn't need another counselor. He's been through them all, and they all focus on the sport and behavior on the ice. But that's not where the problem lies. I think he needs someone like you."

From behind me, Robyn interjects excitedly, "Did you say Zane Ortiz? The star center of the Glaciers?" Kendrick's expression shifts with disapproval at her recognition.

"Yes, that's him. But this is confidential, Robyn. I know you're a hardcore fan. I'm sorry you overheard it," Kendrick says, glancing at Robyn apologetically.

"Again, Kendrick, I'm sorry, it's really not up my alley. If there's any other way I can help—"

"P, can I please talk to you?" Robyn interrupts me.

"Hmm, okay." I eye Kendrick with uncertainty. What does Robyn want to say?

We need to get out of here before Kate and Duke see us.

"Pearl, this is huge!" Robyn's gaze intensifies, and she called me Pearl, a rare occurrence that grabs my attention. "Do you know who Zane Ortiz is?"

"No, I don't. But why would I care? I never work with adults unless they come with their children."

"I get that, but Ortiz is like the rock star of the team. He's as famous as the captain, and if you worked with him, I'd get to meet my favorite hockey player!" Robyn's eyes light up at the thought.

"Girl, that's a tall order for me. You know I'm not into sports," I protest, feeling overwhelmed.

"Will you at least think about it?" she asks gently.

"There isn't much to consider here."

"But...you love helping people," she mumbles, her lower lip quivering slightly.

"I help children who have dealt with trauma. That's my whole career. Not pro athletes. Maybe Kendrick has too much faith in me because of Gabe, but I promise you, I know plenty of good counselors who could help your middle hockey guy."

"Center," Robyn corrects.

"Yeah, same thing. Middle, center. *Tomayto, tomahto.*" I shrug, glancing back at Kendrick, who's still awaiting my response.

When I turn to him to relay the same information, I'm unexpectedly bumped by the couple I was trying so hard to avoid.

"Hey, Coach, great game on Friday," Duke says, patting Kendrick's shoulder.

"Thanks, Duke," Kendrick replies, and my eyes involuntarily roll. Of course, he knows Duke's name. Who isn't smitten by this man?

Kate comes over to hug me. "I couldn't wait to show you the pretty ring Dukey got for me."

Duk-ey. I press my lips together to stifle a gag. Duke doesn't look like a "Duk-ey." I would have never called him that if he'd chosen me.

"That's nice. Congratulations to both of you," I say through gritted teeth, forcing a smile that feels more like a grimace.

"I'm already so overwhelmed with all the preparations," Kate continues.

"So, you've started planning?" I ask, trying to sound casual, though in my opinion, it sounds fast. They should be basking in their newly-engaged bliss.

"Yes, we've been looking at reception venues and all. We want a really small wedding with just a few family members and our close friends from church."

I'm inclined to think I'm not invited because Kate and I aren't the closest of friends. Then she drops the bomb, "I want you to be my bridesmaid. Please say yes?" Her wide smile freezes on her face, and I glance at Robyn. I don't make decisions alone. She either has to ask Robyn too, or I'll graciously decline. "And of course, Robyn. I know she is your other half," Kate adds, clearly not having thought of her initially.

After another exchange with Robyn, silently beseeching her to do this with me, we both accept. When they leave, Kendrick looks at me one last time, his eyes pleading. At this point, I'm only running on adrenaline.

"I can't promise that I'll take him on as my client, but I don't mind meeting him briefly to see if there is anything I can recommend. I'll try to find someone with the expertise that I trust to eventually work with him, but send him to my office."

"That's my girl." Kendrick grins, relief written all over his face.

He must really care about this guy. Kendrick's heart is immense. He and his wife adopted all six of their children when they couldn't have kids. It's a story they love to share, not with a hint of melancholy, but as a testament to how abundantly God has blessed them beyond their wildest dreams.

Just before he leaves, he smoothly pulls out a ticket for next week's game for Robyn, like he's always ready to make someone's day. The next thing I know, she's bouncing around with joy in the church hallway, which still has a few lingering people chatting. Her excitement isn't just about the game; I'm sure it's also because I agreed to meet her favorite player, Zane Ortiz.

4

Pearl Davis

My phone buzzes with a new text message just as I pull into the parking lot outside my apartment. It's Kendrick confirming that his player will be coming to see me on Wednesday. That's the day after tomorrow, and here I am, still clueless about hockey. I don't even know why anyone would want to play the game, let alone how the game is played. Baseball seems like a better fit for me. I wonder why it's not more popular here. And tennis—now that's a game I could get behind, maybe even take my hypothetical future kids to. I detest anything with violence. After dealing with kids who have suffered so much, anything even remotely violent makes my skin crawl.

I'm not sure how I can cram it all in less than two days, but I know exactly who to ask. That's the one and only perk of living with a hockey fanatic.

I step out of the car and into our apartment and I'm immediately struck by how inviting it feels. Robyn and I are now pros at creating a Pinterest-worthy home, although it's more of an obsession of mine than it is for her. There's just something refreshing about walking into our light gray-walled room.

Our living room is just as we like it: beige couches adorned with white, gray, and mustard-colored pillows, a walnut coffee table with a fake plant as the centerpiece, and coffee table books neatly stacked beside it. And no, we don't clutter the space with my horrid psychology books—those are reserved for my office table in my room. Completing the cozy atmosphere are our gray fluffy rug and two crochet blankets that Robyn's mom lovingly made for each of us.

The wall boasts black frames cradling our beloved Bible verses, each set against a pristine white backdrop. My gaze gravitates to mine.

"And we know that for those who love God all things work together for good, for those who are called according to his purpose." Romans 8:28

As I absorb the familiar words, a gentle sense of comfort engulfs me, like a reassuring touch from the Holy Spirit.

Lately, I've been zipping through this room without stopping to think about these verses. I've allowed myself to sink into hurt, swimming in self-doubt and despair and remaining there. My prayers have felt like shouting into the void, but now I'm realizing that I haven't taken the time to actually listen. It's as if the Lord is finally nudging me into stillness, so that I can open my heart and truly hear His voice.

Tears start to flow as I plop down on the floor. I couldn't have planned this moment. My sweater sleeves get damp from all the wiping.

"I'm sorry, Jesus. I'm sorry for not allowing You to comfort me. Forgive me for being so consumed with my own emotions instead of clinging to Your promises. Thank You for reminding me that everything in my life has a purpose known only to You. Thank You for showing me that even in my brokenness, You are working for my good and for Your glory." As I utter these words, it feels like a prayer of repentance. This isn't the first time I've experienced God's grace, but I constantly need a reminder of His unfailing love and mercy.

Growing up in foster homes, with zero sense of identity, belonging to Jesus is the greatest thing that ever happened to me. That's why I chose to become a Christian counselor for kids like me. I want them to find what I found and continue to find on days like these: hope, peace, purpose and the reassurance that they are deeply loved and valued by the King of kings.

I hear the doorknob turn behind me, and Robyn enters. As soon as she sees me on the floor, she drops her bag and kneels to wrap her arms around me. "Do you want to pray about this?"

Her eyes flicker over to me and I can sense her worry, and it's probably because my eyes resemble ripe tomatoes in their crimson hue. Robyn has always been my rock, navigating the craziness of life together. She's been instrumental in my healing journey, especially in these past few weeks when I've been grappling with my feelings for Duke.

We've spent countless moments in prayer for my heart to heal.

With a sniffle, I manage to choke out, "I'm fine, Robs, thank you."

Robyn raises an eyebrow. "You don't look fine. Your eyes are puffy."

"No, really. I just read my life verse, and it felt like God met me right here. I feel comforted. The disappointment lingers, and I'm still sorting through my feelings about Duke and Kate, but I know there's a reason for it all. You were right. Duke wasn't meant for me. What's meant for me, no one can take away."

She beams with pride and claps her hands excitedly. "Praise the Lord. I'm thrilled to see you on the other side of this. But are you sure about being Kate's bridesmaid? You're not obligated to, you know."

"I think I can handle it. It'll just help me see them in a different light. I really want to support and bless them," I reply with a genuine smile, realizing that it's already working. My heart isn't bitter about the thought of them together anymore.

"You're such a sweetheart, P. I'm already wanting to back out, and I didn't even have a crush on her future husband."

I jostle her shoulder, and she teeters to the side, her hands ready to catch her fall. "Too soon to make that joke. "Future husband" makes me feel like I broke the tenth commandment."

"It's not your fault those two met, dated, and got engaged in the span of two months," she says, waving me off.

I laugh at her comment. Robyn has a knack for telling me what I need to hear, whether it's with her blunt honesty or a sprinkle of sweetness.

"Actually, I need your help. Kendrick is sending his player on Wednesday, and I still don't know how many players make a team. Can you teach me everything you know about hockey in less than two days?"

Robyn considers for a moment before responding. "No, I heard Coach saying something about childhood baggage. If he wanted someone with sports expertise, he would have hired a sports counselor. There's a reason he chose you. I trust Coach."

We both settle on the couch, and I playfully swat her with a pillow. "Quit calling him Coach; he's not *your* coach. But seriously, why not? I want to know what I'm diving into with him. It's like reading up on my clients before they show up."

"Normally, I'd be all in for a hockey crash course, but not today. Trust your gut instincts, P. You're really good with people. I reckon you can help him soar without needing to know a puck from a penalty."

I growl in frustration. "I hate feeling unprepared. I might binge-watch a few games to catch up if you're not up for the task."

"Suit yourself. But one thing you should know," Robyn adds with a smirk, "is that Zane Ortiz is easy on the eye."

I stand up and head to my room, dismissing her comment. Handsome men are the last thing on my mind right now.

5
♥

Zane Ortiz

Nothing feels more like home than being on the rink. The sound of skates carving into the ice and sticks clashing resonate in my eardrums, creating a symphony of the sport I love. Coach watches us from the bench, jotting down notes as Tyler leads us through today's practice.

The goal, as always, is to become better with each stride, giving our all and a little bit more. I face off against Trent, our eyes locking in a familiar rivalry that extends beyond the rink. I can feel sweat starting to bead on my brow as I resolve to prove to him once more that he can't beat me on the ice. We engage in a flurry of skill and strategy, maneuvering through his defense with speed and finesse. Okland and Hunter flank me, while Fabrice flashes into position, the puck darting between us like a well-rehearsed routine.

With a swift pass from Fabrice, I find myself in a one-on-one showdown with Carson, one of the best goaltenders I know. But I also know him like the back of my hand, so I anticipate his every move. I deke left, then right, sending him sprawling as I flick the puck into the top corner with a satisfying thud.

The sound of Coach's whistle cuts through the air, signaling the end of the scrimmage. We shake hands and exchange nods of respect, then gather around him for some final notes.

We march through the hallway and the echoes of our footsteps reverberate in loud thuds. From where I'm standing, it's clear that everyone's geared up and eager for Friday's game.

I knock lightly on Coach's office door before heading to the lockers, my mind swirling with thoughts about the therapist he practically strong-armed me into seeing. I've been keeping it out of my mind until today, and now I can't even remember the appointment time.

Coach invites me in.

"I forgot what time the therapist is expecting me," I admit, trying to show Coach I'm making an effort, even if I have no expectations of this therapy session being fruitful.

The possibility of becoming team captain when Tyler leaves is on the table, so I've got nothing to lose by seeing the child therapist—except maybe my precious time and the potential bruising of my ego.

"I scheduled your appointment for 2 p.m. But remember, she usually doesn't see adults or athletes, so she's doing me a favor. Please try your best to open up."

"I can't make no promises, Coach. I'm anything but an open book," I reply with a shrug.

"Try, Ortiz. And please don't be late either. She squeezed us in by a miracle," Coach insists. I wonder if his constant optimism is a requirement for his job, or if he just has a lot of faith in this woman.

"Got it. Can't be fashionably late, then," I quip, but judging by Coach's stern expression, my joke falls flat.

I turn on my heel to leave and Coach stops me with one last piece of advice. "Oh, and make sure you take a good shower before you meet her. It's all about making a good first impression."

I roll my eyes, quite frankly offended. I've never skipped a post-practice shower in my life. In fact, I'm more likely to shower three times a day than not at all.

Why is Coach being so weird about this? I'm going to therapy, not on a date.

I head to the locker room, noticing some of the guys already packing up to leave. I spot an available shower stall and quickly step in and indulge in a thorough cleanse. Coach's words about making a good impression on the therapist echo in my mind. Is he insinuating something about my personal hygiene? Why would he bring it up? I mean, sure I can get ridiculously sweaty but some guys on the team smell far worse than me after a game. But from head to toe, I give myself a good scrub.

My body wash is a citrusy-spicy scent, and by the time I'm done, I almost wish I were going on a date instead of being poked about my issues. I'm never in the mood to explain why I'm just not a happy person.

Stepping out of the shower, I catch Tyler, Fabrice, and Carson eyeing me like there's something on my face. "I would ask why y'all staring like I'm naked, but this is a men's locker room, so that's to be expected," I say with my towel firmly wrapped around my waist. I'll never be one of those guys who don't care about people's comfort levels and strut around Adam-style.

"You never take a twenty-five minute shower here. Are you going on a date?" Carson asks, and I can't help but chuckle.

A date? I haven't had one of those in years. Honestly, I'm not even sure if I remember how to talk to women anymore. Ever since joining the Glaciers, my online presence has blown up. Girls get weird with me, using me for their own social media boost. I've had to end things with many women before the third date because of subtle signs I noticed. The silver lining? I never let anyone get close enough to hurt me.

After being disappointed so many times, I've learned to bail at the first hint of someone being more interested in my status than in me. And now, I don't even have the desire to try anymore. The idea of companionship sounds nice, but I've come to accept that no one will ever truly love me for who I am and, quite frankly, I haven't felt like approaching a woman in a long time. So, I've given up on dating altogether. It just feels like a futile effort.

"We can assume it's a date then since he won't even reply," Fabrice says, high-fiving the guys.

"No, I just have an appointment so I used the shower to think things through," I reply, evading specificity. That's how I like to relate to people. I don't want any of these guys knowing that I'm going to see a therapist. They all respect me on the ice, and I don't want that to change. But I also don't want to explain that I'm doing it for a shot at captaincy. Whenever people mention it, I act like it wouldn't mean the world to me. And lastly, I'm not going to out myself and tell them about Coach's comment about my personal hygiene—that's still not sitting well with me.

"I know what that's like. The shower is one of the best places to talk to God, at least for me. It's the only place I get solitude nowadays," Tyler concedes, and I force a smile, pretending to relate. I don't have four kids under six years old, and I can't even remember the last time I talked to *God*, but I know it's when I was living with my Aunt Melissa in Chicago.

6

Zane Ortiz

I pull onto Main Street and immediately find a spot to park my Audi, grateful that both the therapist's office and my favorite coffee shop are conveniently located here. I usually prefer coming to Randy's around 3 p.m. when the place isn't crowded. It allows me to grab my order and head home without running into fans. As much as I'd love to give Randy's coffee free promotion for their incredible pastries and coffee blends, it's a double-edged sword. It would work in one day, but it would also turn Main Street into a paparazzi camp.

Today, though, I don't have a choice. It's almost 2 p.m., and I can only hope for a semi-uninterrupted trip to the counter. I pull my hat down a bit lower to cover my face and brace myself for all the staring to start.

To my surprise, after the bell rings and I'm inside, there's no typical lunch rush. The café is quiet and only a handful of people are seated and aren't looking in my direction. It seems like I might actually be able to enjoy my coffee in the shop like a normal person without anyone bothering me. Randy, the owner—who's also a fan of mine but promised to keep my presence low-key as long as I frequent his coffee shop—gives me a wide grin as I approach the counter. I give him a nod and order my usual. Danish pastries and an Italian roast.

Today might not be so bad after all.

My heart sinks when the bell rings, and I quickly turn my gaze to the door, expecting a flood of people. Thankfully, it's just one other customer, a woman—though, she's not just any woman. She's stunning, like something out of a dream. I find myself catching my breath, completely unable to tear my eyes away. I want to etch every detail of her beauty into my memory. Her eyes are a mesmerizing shade of forest green, her golden-blonde hair cascades in loose curls, and her petite nose fits perfectly on her round face. And those pink lips...I don't know her but I'm convinced they're naturally full.

She walks toward me and I realize I've been staring like a creep. I blink and turn back to the counter, where my order is ready and waiting for me. Before taking a seat, I notice her uneasy expression and tense posture, probably from my intense gaze. I should apologize, maybe even pretend she reminds me of someone I know. But truthfully, I've never seen anyone quite like her. She's the kind of person you'd want to draw and hang on your wall, and I do draw, though that's beside the point.

She orders without looking at the menu, indicating she's a regular here, and given Randy's smile, he likes her. More points to her for that. We're both regulars. She receives her order, neatly packed in a to-go box, and my heart deflates as she quickly makes her way to the door, clearly attempting to escape my gaze. I commit her last details to memory before she reaches the door. She is wearing beige slacks and a light-pink sweater that perfectly complements her complexion. She effortlessly swings the door open with her forearm, balancing a cup of coffee in one hand and a to-go box in the other. Despite her self-sufficiency, I can't shake the feeling brewing inside me that someone should be there to hold the door for her. Someone like me—yet here I am, frozen in place, captivated by her presence.

What's going on with me? It's weird to feel so strongly about someone I don't even know.

She disappears from view and another sudden urge to follow her tugs at me, tempting me to rise and catch a glimpse of her car and its destination. But that would be crossing into the realm of madness, wouldn't it? I've never felt such an intense curiosity about someone before, let alone a complete stranger. It's absurd, really. Yet I'm still entertaining the idea of playing detective just to satisfy my insatiable desire to know more about her.

It's official—I'm losing my mind.

I manage to keep myself rooted to my seat, resisting chasing after the mysterious woman. Instead, I'm replaying the encounter in the coffee shop over and over again, each moment scorched into my mind. By the time I finally snap out of my reverie, I realize I'm already running late for therapy.

I quickly rise from my seat and tidy up my table, wiping away any remaining crumbs and spills. I also make a mental note to pester Randy later for any information he might have about the enigmatic woman who just graced us with her presence.

·♥·♥·♥·♥·♥·

I knock on the door labeled "Christian Counseling with Davis," the letters neatly printed in elegant script. My mind is still swirling with thoughts of the mystery woman I saw at the coffee shop. A soft voice from within invites me in, and it strikes me as surprisingly youthful.

When I step through the doorway, my heart actually stops.

There she is—the mysterious woman from the coffee shop—sitting in a cozy chair in a room that's more colorful than her outfit. Large windows allow sunlight to pour in, casting a warm glow over her glorious face. I can see how people would feel comfortable opening up in such an inviting environment.

"Please take a seat," she says, her voice almost serenading.

I'm frozen in disbelief. What are the odds that the most out-of-this-world beautiful woman I've ever seen happens to be the therapist who Coach sent me to? It's as if the universe is playing some sort of cosmic joke. Now, Coach's insistence on being showered before the appointment makes sense—though, goodness, this is so surreal.

After a moment, I manage to find a seat, though I'm sure I must look as puzzled as she does right now. There's a starstruck expression on her face that's starting to make my heart drop a little. I had a long list of reasons why therapy wasn't going to work for me, but none of them included the therapist being young, beautiful—and seemingly a fan of mine.

It's not like I dislike my fans or anything. Actually, I appreciate them a lot. They're always there to cheer me on, even when I end up in fights. But when it comes to private interactions, well, I tend to keep my distance. Let's just say I've had my fair share of awkward encounters with many of my female fans.

"So this is when we introduce ourselves. I'm Pearl Davis," she says, her voice a bit shaky but maintaining a professional tone. "And I work with children who have been or are currently in the foster care system. I'd like to get to know you too."

That's it? Just her name and her profession—she seems too young to be a therapist. I wonder how she ended up here. I mean, it's not like this is a date, but I can't help but want to know more about her. Why is she so beautiful? Is she half-angel, half-human? I've heard that's a thing. Not that I believe it, but she'd make me a believer. And those lips... Are they real or just another product of modern cosmetic wonders?

But most importantly, does she enjoy watching me play? If her avoiding my eyes and nervously fidgeting with her crossed legs is any indication, I'd wager that she's feeling the nerves of meeting her favorite player. After all, she works with people all day, so if she wasn't a fan, she wouldn't be this nervous around me. But honestly, she doesn't even need to worry because, for her, I'd sign every picture she's got of me.

"I'm Zane Ortiz. I play with the Glaciers, center position," I reply casually, trying to downplay the fact that I've already gathered so much information in just five minutes of being here.

"Okay, what do you want me to call you?" she asks, her eyes flickering down to her notepad as if contemplating the best way to address me. Maybe she's debating between using my first name or last name. After all, most fans tend to refer to me by my full name.

I shrug. "Zane is fine."

"Great, Zane it is," she chirps, her tone a touch too enthusiastic for the situation. It's almost humorously fake, like she's trying too hard to put herself at ease with this. But hey, at least she's no crazy fan.

7

Pearl Davis

Someone, please, get me some water and open the windows or something. My throat is parched, and the air conditioner seems to be on the fritz, which explains how unbelievably warm this room is. The moment Zane stepped into my office, I knew this session would be anything but ordinary. With his rugged good looks and piercing blue eyes, he resembles more of a movie star than a hockey player. Not that I even know how hockey players look. But I can't bring myself to meet his gaze, afraid that if I do, I'll forget all about being a professional therapist and succumb to the fluttering feeling in my stomach.

It also doesn't help that every inhale is now filled with his intoxicating scent of citrus and spice. It's like being wrapped in a cozy blanket of freshness and warmth, making it impossible not to feel a little lightheaded—in the best possible way.

I can't believe the only heads up Robyn gave me was that he was easy on the eye. In fact, he isn't. Not one bit.

He's the kind of guy who can derail your train of thought by just being in the same room. His muscular frame in a tracksuit and wavy brown hair, along with his chiseled jaw, make me want to lock my eyes on my notepad and never spare him a glance for the rest of my life. And it's not like I just started thinking this now that he's in front of me. When I caught him staring at me at Randy's twenty minutes ago, I wondered why a man as handsome as him was so preoccupied by me. Now, I'm sure he probably did a quick Google search on my practice and recognized me. Props to him; that's more homework than I did.

I had bought a book about hockey history and rules, eager to understand all the ins and outs of the game, despite Coach and Robyn not wanting me to focus on that—I still wanted to know what was coming my way. But I only read five pages before dozing off.

Why am I so backward? I should have also looked him up on social media. But here I am, barely able to keep my voice steady. And the way he's smugly looking at me, it's like he's savoring every moment of my discomfort.

Ugh, I can't let myself be attracted to someone like him.

Is it weird to feel threatened by someone you don't know? He exudes confidence, clearly not used to feeling out of place. But then again, neither am I.

I meet so many parents and children on a daily basis. No one makes me feel out of place in my own office.

I'm not sure why I'm churning like a washing machine in my head, my thoughts are spinning at a speed that could rival a Formula 1 race. Why am I getting so worked up over this? It's just a guy in my office, right? But those few

THE GAME SHE HATES

seconds I allowed myself to get lost in his ocean-blue eyes... I got a feeling he wasn't trying to threaten me.

I have this thing where I judge someone's intentions by their eyes. It's probably weird. But it's worked for me so far, except for a few bumps along the road—namely Duke, Clay...and a few others. Or maybe it didn't work as I like to think.

Back to Zane. He's only here because he needs some help. If he didn't, Kendrick wouldn't have sent him my way. So I'm going to stick to my plan: figure out what he needs and find him a counselor who's the perfect fit. I'm still firm on sticking to my work with children and teens.

"So, Zane," I say, trying to sound composed despite the chaos in my mind. "What brings you to therapy today?"

"Coach thought I needed to see you," he says, his tone casual, but there's a hint of uncertainty in his eyes that tells me he's not entirely convinced Kendrick was wrong to send him my way.

I give a small nod, understanding. "All right. Do you have any idea why *he* thought it was valuable for you to come here?"

He shakes his head.

"Do you want to share with me any negative emotions you've been experiencing lately? This could include feelings of anger, frustration, anxiety, sadness, or anything else that's been on your mind recently."

"I'd say anger, but it's part of the game. So I wouldn't worry about that if I were you," he replies dismissively, his words laced with defiance.

"Do you believe the anger only stems from the game itself, or do you think it's connected to other aspects of your life off the court?"

He snorts in amusement. "You mean off the rink?"

I mentally kick myself for the oversight. I clearly didn't learn much about hockey last night in my book.

"Apologies for the mix-up. Yes, outside the rink," I respond, mustering a smile to cover up my embarrassment.

"I only dish it out on the ice when someone deserves it," he says, his tone tinged with bitterness. "It can easily get ugly there. When losers' only hope for winning is by sending the best players to the penalty box. Someone has to stand up for the team and it's usually me."

My intuition nudges me that the action on the ice might be a coping mechanism for a deeper issue. Taking a leap, I probe further. "Can you share a bit about your childhood and family background?"

"That's not something I like to talk about." His tone is guarded, but I detect a flicker of vulnerability in his eyes.

"I respect that. In therapy, you get to choose what you want to talk about. You don't have to share if you're not ready. But I'm also trying to understand your needs to match you with the right therapist. In case Kendrick didn't mention it, I don't take on clients who aren't below eighteen and haven't been in the foster care system."

His eyes light up in surprise. "You don't want to be my therapist? I thought Coach referred me to you because he thinks you're the only one who can help."

I force a smile. At least he's open to getting help. "Kendrick has faith in me because I worked with his son,

Gabe. But my expertise lies in children that are in the *home*. I can find you someone trained to work with athletes."

"Is there nothing I can do to convince you to keep me with you?" He wiggles his eyebrows suggestively, and I can't believe my eyes.

"We're still talking about therapy, right?" I reply, keeping my tone nonchalant.

"Yeah, of course. Unless you want to talk about something else." He smirks, testing the waters, but he'll need to try harder if he wants to break through my professionalism.

"I'm sorry again. I can't work with you. You need to trust me on this. It's in your best interest to see someone who specializes in working with adults."

"Fair. Can I at least have your number?"

I definitely saw that one coming and simply reply, "I'm sorry, Zane. You may not have my personal number, but you can always call my office."

"But why? It's not like you're going to be my therapist, right?"

"I know, but it's still not a good idea. Anyway, I will need your permission to share my notes from today's session, which will be beneficial for the referral process."

"Do I have access to those notes?"

I nearly chuckle at the question. There isn't much he gave me to work with. "You do. It's like your health records. They are primarily yours."

When our awkward conversation reaches a stalemate, I decide it's time to end the session before he tries any harder to break through my professional walls. "Well, it looks like our time is up. I have another family coming in soon, and I need to prepare."

He gives me a wide grin and gets up. "I will see you again soon."

Not if I have anything to say about it.

I smile back, relieved when he finally exits my office. It's the first time my shoulders relax since Zane Ortiz's appointment started. I couldn't have endured it if this were a typical, full-length appointment and not just a brief introductory meeting—being in the room with him felt so suffocating.

8

Zane Ortiz

Thoughts of Pearl dancing through my mind are making my return back home the most exhilarating non-game-related drive ever. It's amusing and downright adorable to recall the myriad of expressions she displayed, each one an attempt to maintain composure.

At one point, I started wondering if she's truly a fan of mine, considering how adeptly she concealed that tidbit. She wasn't too thrilled with my probing questions and offbeat comments, and it just made it hard for me to figure her out. Despite her still being a mystery to me, I could certainly tell she genuinely likes helping others, and she's found a way to channel that passion through her profession.

I may have acted disappointed when she refused to be my therapist, but it was all part of my plan. Now that she's not my therapist, there's a chance to get to know her on a more personal level. And let me tell you, she's the most intriguing person I've ever met. The way she furrowed her brows in thought, pursed her lips in anticipation of my responses, and twiddled nervously while her gaze remained fixed on her notepad—every detail is ingrained in my memory.

A chuckle escapes me as I pull into my garage, still thinking about her.

It's never been my experience to encounter a woman who didn't throw herself at me like a puck at a goal, vying for my attention. Pearl may be a fan, but she's different—refreshingly so. The thought of getting to know her beyond the confines of a therapist's office ignites a fire within me, propelling me to pursue her with all the fervor of a playoff game.

I cringe as I realize how absurdly passionate my thoughts sound. My views on women and love haven't shifted overnight, but I also can't deny the magnetic pull she has on me.

I burst through the door and toss my keys on the dining table as I make a beeline for my trusty Xbox. I flop on the couch, grab the controller and dive headfirst into the world of *Call of Duty*. It's my go-to escape, and right now, I need it more than ever to take my mind off Pearl. Living alone in this big house I bought when I signed with the Glaciers definitely has its perks, but it can get lonely at times. Still, I'd choose a night in over the chaos of the bar scene any day.

My house, nestled in a peaceful neighborhood, features high ceilings, tiled floors, and a grand staircase that curves around leather sofas near a modern fireplace. It's a far cry from the chaotic environment I grew up in, with my dad's alcohol abuse that caused emotional turmoil from my early days. That's why I steer clear of parties and post-game celebrations; I'd rather not risk falling into the same destructive patterns. I always fear that addiction lurks in my genes, and I don't want to find out. Tyler and Carson aren't party animals either, but for different reasons.

Still, when it comes to bonding, the team comes together whether it's watching a game or hitting the gym. I genuinely enjoy hanging out with most of them off the ice, even though I might not always show it. Well, except for Trent—he just can't seem to quit with his snarky comments directed at me.

The gunfire in the game slows down and my thoughts drift back to Pearl. I pause it and pull out my phone, quickly searching for "Pearl Davis" online. There it is—her practice, with nothing but five-star ratings and glowing reviews. I devour every word.

I feel like I'm getting to know her in a way I never did during our session today; she seemed so guarded. She's described as kind, attentive, respectful, conversational, genuine, comforting, and she loves working with kids, among other praises.

There's still so much more I want to know.

I zoom in on her professional photo, studying her features in detail. There's something unique about her, something that's really special and draws me in. Yet, even as I stare at her picture, it pales in comparison to the genuine presence and warmth I experienced earlier.

I switch gears and try to find her on social media. But it's like she's a ghost—there's nothing, not even a hint of her personal life. Frustrated, I madly toss my phone to the end of the couch, my heart skipping a beat as it almost hits the floor. I can't afford to break my screen twice in the same month.

It's baffling—in this age, where we have so much information at our fingertips, how can she be this hard to find?

The sound of my phone ringing cuts through my game and I instinctively assume it's Coach checking in on how therapy went, or maybe one of the guys wanting to shoot the breeze. But when I glance at the screen, it's Aunt Melissa's name flashing. My heart jolts.

I hesitate, my first instinct not to answer—it's become almost routine to let her calls go to voicemail. But each time I do, a twinge of guilt gnaws at me. Aunt Melissa is my mom's only sister, and for as long as I can remember, she's been relentless in her efforts to get closer to me, to treat me like her own. But I've kept her at arm's distance, for two reasons.

First, I never knew my mom, and Aunt Melissa is the closest connection I have to her. She puts into perspective a connection I should've had with my own mother but never got the chance to experience. And second, how could I accept her affection when the man who should have loved me most never did? It's been hard to let her in, to fully believe in her affection. I've pushed her away for years, but she's never stopped trying.

Now, as I've grown older and started to believe that maybe she does love me, it feels like it's too late to reciprocate. That's why I haven't been back to Chicago since I moved to Bedford.

THE GAME SHE HATES

The phone stops ringing, and another prick of conscience tightens in my chest. I know all she wants is to check on me, to ask how I'm doing. And for some reason, I decide I owe it to her to do better this time.

I call her back, and the phone rings just once before she picks up. "Hi, Aunt Mel, sorry for missing your call earlier," I say, feeling shame.

"Zane, sweetheart, I can't believe you called me back," she responds, her voice brimming with warmth and affection. I wince at the truth of what she said.

"You know how it is, hockey keeps me busy," I repeat the same excuse I've used even during the off-season.

"I know, I know. But I just need to know how you're doing sometimes. I even watch your games to catch a glimpse of you. I miss you."

It's hard to imagine someone thinking about me, missing me. But Aunt Mel is probably not lying; I just struggle to accept her affection.

"Thanks for watching my games. I'll try to visit when I can." I surprise even myself with the promise.

"Zane, is this a promise?" she asks, hope lacing her tone.

"It is." I may be elusive, but I'm still a man of my word.

"Zane," Aunt Mel continues, her tone shifting slightly. "Have you been thinking about next month?"

April. The month I've dreaded ever since Dad's DUI charge ten years ago that resulted in severe injuries for the family he ran into. I'd hoped they'd lock him up for life—he deserved it after all the convictions that were stacked against him over the years. Yet, here we are, ten years later, and his release looms on the horizon. I push aside the anger and resentment simmering within, refusing to let it consume me.

"I haven't. I don't want to think about it," I admit, my voice stuck in my throat.

"You'll have to, Zane. I know it's incredibly hard, but so much can change in ten years."

"Nothing can ever change that man, Aunt Mel." I don't care if she hears the bitterness seeping into my words. It's my cue to end this call before she launches into her usual spiel about second chances and redemption. I still don't know how she managed to visit my dad knowing how much hurt he brought in my life. "I've got to go make dinner. It's getting late, and I haven't eaten anything."

When it comes to my dad, I can't bring myself to believe in miracles. He's had a hundred chances, and he's squandered them all on his addiction, which was the source for all the pain he's inflicted on others. His release next month doesn't change a thing—a few months down the line, he'll be back behind bars, where he belongs.

9

Pearl Davis

I'm reading a cozy mystery book while sitting on the couch, but my mind is fixated on the door, waiting for Robyn to come in so I can give her a piece of my mind. If she hadn't insisted on me seeing Zane in front of Kendrick, none of today's embarrassment would have happened.

The sound of the lock turning draws my full attention to the door.

Robyn bursts in energetically. "I've never been more excited to come home. My best friend met my hockey hero. Spill, tell me everything."

I just shoot her a pointed glare.

"What's wrong? You look like you're ready to tear into me. Did I do something?"

"You bet you did. In fact, you did a lot wrong. Who sends their best friend into the lion's den without a warning?" I throw my hands up in exasperation.

"What on earth are you talking about?" Robyn's brow furrows in confusion.

"You know exactly what I'm talking about, Robs."

"Oh no, is this about Zane Ortiz? Is he fierce off the ice too? I thought his aggression was confined to the rink and the *other* teams always start the fights. Did he say or do something to you?"

I roll my eyes. The Zane I met couldn't be further from aggressive. I can't even imagine him getting into a scuffle, but I can certainly see him charming every woman in sight.

"You didn't prepare me for what he looks like."

She giggles. "Oh, I warned you all right. I said he was pleasant to look at or something like that."

"Robs, you said he was easy on the eye, and maybe on the ice he is. But in person, he looks like a menace to women trying to find their godly men. And worst of all, *he knows it*." I almost gag as memories of his stubborn smirk and less-than-cute lopsided grin come to mind.

Robyn squeals. "Goodness, P. Are you crushing on Zane Ortiz? Don't worry; there's an entire online fan club swooning over him. You're not the only one falling for his charm. Bedford is full of women like you."

"Me? Crushing on a hockey player? You have the wrong number. I mean, sure, he looks like a model and movie star combined, but he's a predator. I hated every minute he was in my office," I exaggerate, trying to make a point. I did enjoy his scent; that was nice. But it was also threatening, drawing me closer. But that wasn't intentional. Or at least I don't think it was. Every comment, the way his gaze pierced me—it was all torture. I wish I had never laid eyes on him.

"Did you get hit on by Zane Ortiz?" Robyn fans herself, biting her lower lip. "I'm gonna scream. I'm gonna lose it. *Lose it*," she singsongs.

"He tried to get my number. It was so annoyingly predictable."

"So, this doesn't sound like a therapy session if you're telling me all this."

I huff and shake my head. "He can't be my client. For all the reasons I told you and Kendrick last time, and now, on top of that, he's danger incarnate."

"You've been hit on by your clients, clients' parents, and some really handsome men. Why are you so worked up over Zane? You're not even a fan of his. Do you maybe think you felt something for him?"

"Robs, drop that thought right now. I've dated enough pretty faces to know better than to give someone like him a second thought. I kept it professional the whole time."

"Are you saying I can kiss my dreams of meeting Zane Ortiz goodbye?"

"Absolutely. Forget about it because I'll make sure we never have to see each other again." I rise from my chair and make my way to the kitchen. Dinner isn't going to cook itself.

"You non-hockey fans are such grumps," Robyn shouts after me.

I roll my eyes. Robyn thinks she's invincible to heartache because she's never fallen for anyone who could break her heart. She can't possibly understand what it was like to meet Zane. It wasn't just about his looks; there was something about him that drew me in, something I managed to resist only by the skin of my teeth.

·♥·♥·♥·♥·♥·

After two successful sessions with my clients and a meeting with a social worker, it's already lunchtime, which means Randy's customary coffee and danish—or perhaps today I'll opt for a scone. I often ponder whether I should make healthier lunch choices, but then I remind myself that my regular living room workouts grant me permission to indulge in a treat every day.

I stroll down the street to my favorite coffee shop, and the welcoming chime of bells greet me as I enter. Joining the queue, I take a moment to check my phone. While I'm not active on social media platforms, I do participate in a church group and often receive updates on the week's activities and messages from the youth ministry that I sometimes lead.

Out of nowhere, a familiar husky voice startles me from behind. "It's your turn now," Zane's voice rings out. I jump in surprise, turning to find him wearing a baseball cap, sunglasses, and an all-black outfit straight out of a magazine.

"What's your deal looking like a robber?" I tease, masking the fact that seeing him sends my heart racing.

"Trying to blend in and avoid attention." This explains his choice of shades indoors but he's got it all wrong, black makes such a statement. I'm surprised he doesn't know this.

"If you don't want to stand out, you should try neutral colors," I suggest, motioning to my own champagne jumpsuit. I don't typically do bright colors either, but my office is an exception—I want it to be inviting, especially for the children who come to process their thoughts with me.

I quickly realize how absurd it is that I'm fixating on his incognito outfit choices. This is the second time we've accidentally bumped into each other here, and today feels less like a coincidence.

I turn back from placing my order with Randy and glare at him. "What are you even doing here?"

He raises his arms in mock surrender. "This is a public place, you know. You're making it sound like I broke in or something."

I give him another once-over to remind him that his outfit doesn't exactly scream *innocent bystander.*

"I'm here at Randy's every single day around this time, and I've never once spotted you."

Zane just shrugs. "Happy coincidence. I come here often too."

I raise an eyebrow. "Is this where you come to take selfies with your fans?"

He quickly gestures for me to lower my voice and steps closer, setting off alarms in my head. That scent again—citrus and spice. I instinctively take a step back, only to be stopped by the counter. I can't handle any more of this.

"What?" I ask.

"I don't like to be seen in public. It creates chaos. Can we sit in that corner?" he asks, indicating a secluded spot where he was likely sitting, a coffee already on the table.

I feign glancing at my watch. "I have to get back to my office."

"Can I at least walk you back?" he insists, his eyes hopeful.

"No need, it's just around the corner," I reply with a forced grin, eager to make my escape as soon as possible.

His smile falters for a moment, but he quickly recovers. "I just wanted to ask about my referral. Maybe we can talk about it later over dinner?" he suggests *too* casually.

The audacity of this guy! He's clearly not used to being told no, but I refuse to be another notch on his belt.

"I'll let you know as soon as I find you someone," I say through pursed lips. "I'll need you to trust me on this."

"I trust you, Sweet P. I just need you to trust me too and let me take you to dinner." He flashes me with his charming smile that leaves me breathless for a moment.

Wait what. "How do you know my nickname? Did Robs talk to you?"

"Your nickname is Sweet P?" He facepalms himself. "And I thought I coined a unique name for you. Who is Robs? Your boyfriend?"

I roll my eyes, growing tired of his games, and grab my order and stride past him, ignoring his pleas to meet for coffee tomorrow. As I walk to the door, I can feel his eyes boring into my back, but I refuse to let him see how much he's rattled me.

Back in my office, I sink onto the couch, replaying the awkward encounter in my mind. I can't understand why he's so fixated on me when there's a queue of girls obsessed with him. It frustrates me how he revels in making me squirm, but I won't give him the satisfaction of seeing me crack. He'll tire of this game long before I do.

10
♥

Zane Ortiz

"Earth to Ortiz!" Carson's voice breaks through my haze, snapping me back to reality. I blink and quickly realize that my hands have been absentmindedly sharpening my skates for tomorrow's game, but my thoughts could not be further away.

"You've been off today, man. Everything okay?"

The whole team sensed something off about my performance on the ice. Usually, I glide effortlessly, but my mind wasn't in practice today. Every stride felt forced, every move unnatural. It's not like me to struggle with feeling sluggish while skating.

"Everything's fine. Just got a few things on my mind," I reply, brushing off his concern. I don't want to burden him with my thoughts, especially about a girl.

"Missing that many shots ain't like you, Ortiz," Carson says with a frown. He's right. Losing focus on the ice isn't me. And getting distracted by a woman who doesn't seem interested?

Definitely not me.

"It won't happen again," I assure him with a tight-lipped smile.

"It better not. We need you back on your A-game tomorrow." He taps my shoulder, jolting me back to the present once again.

Tyler calls us in for a team huddle, discussing game strategy against tomorrow's opponent. Yet, my mind is stuck replaying my encounters with Pearl. It's getting ridiculous how much space she occupies in my thoughts, especially when she seems to want nothing to do with me.

I can't wrap my head around why she's keeping me at arm's length. Randy mentioned she's a regular during lunchtime, so I broke my rule and waited for her, risking being noticed for over an hour, just for her to dismiss me. It's frustrating to put in that effort only to be met with indifference. All I wanted was a chance to get to know her. She's been intriguing from the moment I laid eyes on her. How is showing interest not a compliment to a woman?

I initially thought her hesitance was because of our professional relationship, but now that there's none, I'm just confused.

She's definitely a tough nut to crack—every interaction feels like a puzzle I can't solve. There's this inviting aura about her, and she seems to want to help me and is committed to finding the right therapist for me. That level of dedication is something I can't help but admire. That's why I mentioned the referral today, even though I'm not exactly enthusiastic about counseling. But if it means she'll think about me, even just a little, I'll keep that thread going.

For the first time in my life, my interest in a woman has been genuinely piqued, and I don't know how to pull back.

There's something about her that makes every stumble worth it. If she's playing hard to get, count me in. I'll match her move for move and I'll enjoy every minute of the chase. And if she's guarding her heart from another potential heartbreak, I'll be right there to prove that I'm not like those other guys. I'll be the one who brings a smile, not tears.

What I know for sure now is that she's definitely not a fan of mine, or even of the Glaciers for that matter. But strangely, none of that seems to faze me. I'm more than willing to seek her out, even if she's cheering in an opposing team's jersey. Although I'd like nothing more than to see her in my jersey, even just for a moment, to experience the rush it would bring.

"Are you with me, man?" Tyler's concern pierces through his eyes as he turns to me. I nod, though inwardly I'm anything but.

I join the chant as we pump ourselves up and get fired up for tomorrow's game.

Coach pulls me aside and asks in a low voice. "Wanna tell me what's going on in that head of yours?"

"Nothing, Coach. Just a rough day. I'm all focused for tomorrow's game," I reply loudly, trying to dispel any doubts anyone might have. I'd never let my crazy thoughts cost us a game. It's frustrating, though, to realize that a woman has this much power over me.

No one has ever had this effect on me.

"Whatever it is, you know you can always talk to me. I know Pearl is looking for another therapist for you. I was sad to hear she didn't change her mind about working with you," Coach mentions, and I can't help but wince at the mention of Pearl.

Not only does she not want to work with me, but she also doesn't want to spend even a minute talking to me in public.

I nod, appreciating Coach's concern. He's always been invested in my personal life and has been aware of my family history from the start. He tries to support me whenever he can. But I wonder if his kindness stems from a sense of obligation as my coach, or if it genuinely comes from a place of care.

That's the problem with me. I find it difficult to simply accept people's kindness at face value. I spend more time than necessary trying to dissect their motives.

11
♥

Zane Ortiz

The entire team gathers in Tyler's kitchen for dinner. It's a tradition we have—the night before every game, we share a meal as a team. It's not just about the food; it's a bonding ritual that helps us stay connected and accountable, particularly for the more adventurous souls among us. It's reassuring to know that we all headed home early afterward, and we'll all be well-rested and ready for the game.

I eye the salmon on my plate, eager to dig in and savor the delicious meal Lacey, Tyler's wife, has prepared. Her cooking is always spot on—nutritious and bursting with flavor. Despite the chaos the team brings to her home, she doesn't seem to mind. Unlike some of the other wives who often find us too loud, she's always happy to have us over for dinner.

I scan the dining table and notice Trent and Gus sitting next to the only empty spot. Without hesitation, I decide to avoid Trent and head for the balcony instead. Tyler, Carson, and Fabrice are already out there, enjoying the evening breeze. I take a seat on a stool next to Tyler, surrounded by his energetic kids who are trying their best to negotiate their way out of bedtime.

Being around Tyler's kids always brings back memories of my own childhood. Seeing their innocence and vitality, I feel a stab in my chest, remembering a time when I didn't feel loved or cared for. My dad's mess dragged me down, and the only relief I found was when Aunt Melissa would take me away for a few months. But then my dad would come back, claiming me for government benefits, and the cycle would repeat.

For years, I viewed kids as a burden because my dad constantly reminded me that I was nothing more than a drain on his resources. As a child, he made it clear that my opinions didn't matter because I was incapable of grasping adult concepts. From the moment I was born, I was an unending wellspring of pain and misery in his eyes. His words left scars that ran deep, and it had shaped the belief that I never wanted to bring a child into this world to endure the same suffering.

But watching Tyler with his kids has opened my eyes to what a loving, involved father looks like. His four children adore him, and he showers them with care and attention, even calls them after every game and practice. The pride he takes in their smallest accomplishments never fails to amaze me.

My neglectful father led me to believe that all dads were inherently flawed, but Tyler has proven me wrong. Maybe one day I'll be ready to embrace the joy of fatherhood myself and adopt a few mini hockey players of my own.

"Uncle Zane, do you want to see the giraffe Daddy painted in my room?" Tia asks, beaming with excitement. She's almost six and Tyler's firstborn.

I nod. "Of course. I'd love to see it," I reply, with a hint of sarcasm toward Tyler. I didn't peg him as the artistic type.

"Tia, darling, maybe you don't want to show Uncle Zane because he thinks his drawings are better than Daddy's since he's an artist," Tyler says.

I flash him a modest smile. I don't consider myself an artist, but drawing was my first therapy before I stepped foot on the ice.

"No, Daddy, your drawing is the best. He needs to see the pink giraffe!" Tia insists.

A laugh escapes my lips. I quickly rise to my feet. I'm eager to see this pink giraffe.

"I want to see it, Tia." I turn back to Tyler. "Pink? Really, Captain?" I say quietly, raising an eyebrow at him.

Tia leads me to her room, her two younger sisters following along. Each wall is covered with Tyler's artwork, and though the art is questionable, their happiness and love for it are undeniable.

"You're not allowed to make fun of me in my own house," Tyler jokes as he enters the room. The girls slip out, probably in search of another audience for their dad's artwork.

"You know, you could've just asked. I could've turned these rooms into something straight out of Disney," I jest, flashing a grin.

"You would've?" Tyler asks, a skeptical edge in his voice.

"Absolutely! Why wouldn't you think I'd be up for it?" I reply, feeling a bit offended. Tyler has only been kind to me and I thought we had a solid friendship, religion aside.

"It's just that you like to keep to yourself a lot. I wouldn't dream of burdening you with such a time-consuming project."

I rub the back of my neck, feeling a bit uneasy. My teammates might assume I don't care about them off the ice, but that couldn't be further from the truth. "I may not show it, but I really value being part of the Glaciers. And you're all like..." I hesitate, unable to bring myself to say "family." The word feels foreign, given my upbringing with my dad and my struggles to accept Aunt Melissa's love.

"Friends," I finally settle on.

"I understand you had it rough growing up, but sometimes, God provides us with new opportunities to fill the voids from our past. You've undoubtedly made many of us better players through your tactics and resilience. I have no doubt that you enjoy being part of the team. But, I hope you'll consider letting us into the parts of your life that you've kept closed off. You don't have to open up to everyone, just to a few people you trust and believe will support you. Life isn't just about hockey, and I sure know that because I'm retiring. I believe there's something even greater waiting for me beyond the rink." Tyler pauses, letting his words sink in, but I struggle to imagine a life where hockey isn't my everything.

"What could be better than playing hockey professionally? I thought you were making a sacrifice for your family?"

Tyler's smile widens. "I don't see it as a sacrifice. Hockey has never been an idol for me; it's been a profession, for a season of my life. My primary purpose is to be a godly husband and father to my kids. Whatever profession I have serves my family first and foremost. Now, with all the kiddos we have and my wife homeschooling, hockey is pulling me away from the people I love most. But that's just my story. Even those who cling to hockey into their forties eventually have to hang up their skates. Then what?"

His words hit me like a ton of bricks. At twenty-eight, the thought of life after hockey had never crossed my mind. Maybe because I loathed my life before hockey—this life is the only good life I know.

"I've never even considered not playing."

"You don't have to completely stop. You can coach, play with your kids. But professionally, it's just for a season. It's good to think about life after this once in a while."

I chuckle in disbelief.

"You don't plan on having any kids?"

"I'm not sure. I had a really awful dad."

"You never know what's in store for you. Both my wife and I didn't come from stable backgrounds, but encountering the love of Jesus changed everything for us. Our lives now are like night and day compared to how we grew up. Your past doesn't have to define your future, especially when you accept Christ as your Lord and Savior. It's like becoming a whole new person, and the change is reflected everywhere, even within the dynamics of your family."

Talking to Tyler is always pleasant until his words start feeling like they're in a different language, one I struggle to understand, especially when he brings religion into the conversation. I admire how he credits his faith for his success, but the idea that it could be anyone's story if they wanted never fails to baffle me.

"Hey, guys. Everyone's going home. I wanted to say a little prayer before tomorrow's game," Lacey announces from the door. I'm grateful for the interruption, as I have nothing to add to Tyler's last words.

I quickly make my way out, and Lacey leads us in a prayer for safety and success in the game, and for our opponents to *know* Jesus through playing with us.

After we exchange goodbyes and head home, I find myself pondering what it would be like to have the same faith Tyler's family has and live for something bigger than myself. Something that illuminates even the darkest corners of my life with an inextinguishable hope.

12
♥

Pearl Davis

Boy, was I wrong about this bridesmaids meeting. I thought the hardest thing about joining the girls today would be enduring endless chatter about how Kate met Duke and their impending happily-ever-after. I even said a little prayer before coming here, to maintain a cheerful spirit. Little did I know that everyone would be so focused on watching the Glaciers and Falcons game.

If I had known it was going to turn into a hockey night, I would've gladly opted for a cozy evening alone in my apartment. Of course, Robyn had the perfect excuse to skip out on this meeting with her coveted ticket to the game. The way she flashed that ticket at me, it was clear she'd miss the Glaciers game when pigs fly. If only I had a similarly convincing excuse. Unfortunately, I'm known for never bailing on anything, and Kate would've undoubtedly pulled out all the stops to ensure I show up.

Summoning a burst of courage, I make another attempt to divert their attention. The small living room is packed with Becky, Sarah, and Lydia, all from our church and part of the worship team, along with Nadine, who's Kate's cousin and roommate, also seated on the carpet. Stepping in, I observe their faces, glued to the TV screen, completely absorbed in the game. Sarah and Becky react with animated gestures at different points of the game, while Kate gasps in disbelief, exclaiming "that was a close call" each time. Nadine is passionately shouting at what I assume is the opposing team. It's only then that I notice Lydia's jersey—it has "Ortiz" written at the top with the number 12 in bold white font. Could that be Zane's number? The chances of it being another player with the same last name seem slim.

A twinge of tension grips me, though I can't quite pinpoint why. Robyn already filled me in about Zane's status as one of the best players, with a legion of devoted fans—many of them women who are utterly infatuated with him.

I hope Lydia is simply wearing his jersey for admiration of his skills on the ice.

I gaze at the screen and try to spot him amidst the flurry of players darting across the ice at lightning speed. Is this even safe? The way they move seems almost unreal. I've never set foot on ice, let alone attempted skating at that speed; the thought of sharp blades beneath my feet sends shivers down my spine. I've always been a practical footwear kind of girl. I never stray beyond a 2-inch heel for safety's sake.

"So, is the game almost finished?" I interject, breaking the silence, and all eyes turn to me.

"Do you really hate hockey?" Kate asks in disbelief.

"I never said I hated it." It's funny how people always assume that if you're not into a sport they love, it means you must hate it.

"Well, we heard Robs say something like that," the girls tease.

"I've just never been into any sports."

"How can you not enjoy this?" Lydia asks. Something about the fact that she is wearing a jersey with Zane's name on it gives me the itch.

Why do I always feel possessive over men who aren't even mine? First Duke, and now Zane. Something is seriously wrong with me because I don't even like Zane at all. He gives me the itch too.

"It's too violent and way too fast-paced for me. I don't know what's happening," I deadpan.

"Well, if we're being honest, I only care about two things: Zane Ortiz and for the Glaciers to win. So, I'm really not paying attention to everything else that's happening either," Lydia admits.

My stomach churns at the mention of Zane's name.

"Why Zane? Does he play better than everyone else?" I ask, feigning nonchalance.

"No, Collymore is the greatest defenseman the world has ever seen. And that jawline—pure perfection. A pity he is retiring," Becky swoons.

"Sorry, I'll have to side with Lydia here," Nadine adds. "Sarah, could you pull up the Glaciers' socials and show us Zane in his full glory? Those piercing eyes, that chiseled body, that smile. And the way he never shies away from a good on-ice scuffle. I'm all in for Team Zane Ortiz."

I'm officially irritated now. Lord, help me. I can't seem to keep my emotions in check, and I know whatever I'm feeling isn't valid in any way.

"I like having my eyes on Adler. Carson Adler. He might not be everyone's top pick, but there's something about him that just speaks to me. I like to think that one day I'll meet him and have the chance to tell him how special he is," Sarah says in a dreamy voice.

"Girls, stop it. We're here to enjoy the game, not to ogle the players. Remember, some of them have wives and families," Kate interrupts. Makes total sense. She's fully engaged and not interested in this conversation.

"We're actually here for a bridesmaids meeting, Kate. I think we should get to it," I remind everyone in case they forgot why we're *really* here.

Kate winces. "Sorry, Pearl. This game is halfway. Can you try and sit it through, and we'll make today's meeting short?"

I suppress the urge to roll my eyes as I reluctantly agree. Grabbing a bar stool from the island, I settle back into watching the game. My gaze returns to the TV screen, scanning for number 12—I manage to spot him for a few seconds before the camera shifts to other players.

Zane scores a goal, prompting all the girls to erupt in cheers and high-five each other. As the camera zooms in for the replay, I finally get a full view of his face in slow motion. He's unarguably handsome even behind a full face shield, and with all the confidence he exudes, along with his persistence from yesterday, I'm certain he's well aware of his heartthrob reputation.

The game progresses, and I find myself secretly thrilled, particularly when I catch a glimpse of number 12 out on the ice. It's as if I'm playing my own private game—tracing his movements across the rink. Though I'm sure Lydia is doing the same.

I still can't understand the players' willingness to risk injury for a puck. Still, I admire their fearlessness. Fear is something I grapple with every day, so it's intriguing to imagine being on the other side of it.

The girls' voices ring out in unison, echoing disbelief and frustration. "Seriously? They're penalizing Zane for that? It was a clean play!" The atmosphere instantly tenses up. I catch Zane's visibly angry expression on TV, but I'm clueless about what actually happened.

I hesitate to ask what's happening. Revealing any interest in the game would contradict my earlier stance, and I definitely don't want to be roped into more game nights. Yet, the urge to know what the referee said to Zane and the repercussions he faces consumes my thoughts.

13

Zane Ortiz

The adrenaline courses through my veins and my heart pounds in my chest. I feel my blood boiling as I shoot a glare at the referee, my frustration barely contained. With clenched fists and gritted teeth, I argue my case, attempting to reason with the official before begrudgingly making my way to the penalty box.

"I was just trying to defuse the situation," I mutter to myself. It's Wood who's at fault here—he instigated the skirmish near the Falcon's goal crease. When he turned aggressive toward Hunter, I stepped in and pushed him away. But when Wood attempted to put me in a headlock, instinct took over, and I reacted by shoving him into the plexiglass. Yet, somehow, the referee twisted the narrative, painting me as the instigator.

I take my seat in the penalty box, my hands trembling with nerves and anger. It's not just about me; it's about the team. With us in the third period, leading 3-2, being short a center could give the Falcons the opening they need to catch up.

With each passing moment, the tension mounts, the crowd holding its breath as the players fight tooth and nail for every inch of ice.

In a climactic moment, the final buzzer echoes through the arena, marking the end of the game. I spring up from the bench. It's finally over.

Although tonight's hard-earned victory carries a hint of lingering anger, I can't help but join in the celebration with the team.

In the aftermath of the game, the locker room crackles with what I can only describe as testosterone-fueled energy. Some teammates head straight for the showers, steam rising as they wash away the intensity of the match. Others are stretching tired muscles and reliving key plays and near misses.

Meanwhile, a couple of us are tending to minor injuries under the watchful eye of the team's medical staff. They patch us up nicely. We'll be back in top form in no time.

I'm sitting on the bench, a cold pack soothing my tired legs, when I sense a looming presence in front of me. Trent's voice cuts through the locker room chatter like a blade, his words dripping with accusation. "What were you thinking, man? You nearly cost us this one."

Great, just as I was starting to forget the ref's wrong call on the penalty. Trent's words feel like another dagger to the wound. Coach and the rest of the team didn't say a word. Everyone saw it. It wasn't my fault. I was just trying to defend myself and Hunter.

"I did my part tonight, Trent," I say, my voice steady but my fists clenched at my sides, just in case. I rise to my feet, meeting his gaze head-on, but I refuse to engage in a pointless argument. He's just a bully, stuck in some high school power play, and I won't let him drag me into it.

I begin to walk away and Trent follows closely behind. "You weren't yourself at practice yesterday. And you acted out again today. The team is just tired of having to carry the weight of your anger issues."

Before I know it, I've turned around to face him, our faces inches apart. He is a few inches shorter, but still a tall guy on the team. I can feel everyone's eyes on us. I can't do something I might regret. Captaincy is on the table.

"You and who, Trent? Who else feels like they're having to carry my weight?" The silence that follows is deafening, no one daring to speak up. Maybe it's because I scored two goals tonight, or maybe they don't want to admit that Trent's just blowing smoke.

I let out a frustrated huff. "That's what I thought. I won't be bullied by you, okay?"

Suddenly, Tyler steps in and puts his hand on my shoulder as he turns me away from Trent's imposing figure. "Ortiz, you've gotta stop letting people like Trent get under your skin, man," he whispers. "The team believes in you. We all saw what happened on the ice. You could have chosen not to go after that guy, but he was trying to put you in a headlock because he knew you wouldn't give up. None of us fault you tonight. And Trent knows it too. He's just worked up by the fact that you'll be captain once I hang up my skates."

My anger begins to simmer. Coach hasn't said anything definitive to me about being captain. "You think I'll get to be the team's captain?" I ask, cautiously optimistic.

"I think you could be. Coach and management are still deciding among all the alternates, but my vote goes to you. And I know they'll see it too. But you also have to do your part in bringing the team together, not apart."

I sigh. He's right—I need to step up and be a leader on and off the ice. But ignoring Trent's constant bullying is easier said than done.

· ♥ · ♥ · ♥ · ♥ · ♥ ·

Once again, I plan to wait here until the sweet Pearl graces me with her presence. Despite my hopeful outlook, the crowd of people inside Randy's café is making me nervous. I've been lucky to go unnoticed twice before, but today may look different.

I've taken Pearl's advice to heart and dressed in gray sweats, hoping to blend in and avoid her labeling me a robber—unless, of course, it's her heart that I'm stealing.

I approach Randy with sunglasses and the hoodie pulled low, partially covering my face.

He greets me with a wide smile. "Good game yesterday. I loved every minute until they wronged you."

"Don't even remind me. I'm still salty about that call," I reply, feeling the frustration all over again.

"Ahh, don't worry about it. It always happens to the best players." He rubs his chin thoughtfully. "So, it seems you've changed your usual time here, Tizer." That's his quirky nickname for me to keep my identity incognito.

I return his smile. "I figured there's no harm in coming here during your peak hours if I disguise myself properly."

He shakes his head. Of course, Randy sees through my feeble excuse for changing my hours; his narrowed eyes say it all. "I know the therapist is why you changed your hours." He leans in and adds in a hushed tone, "I can't promise you won't be spotted, though. Lunchtime can get pretty hectic around here. You've got to hope everyone's too focused on their phones to notice you."

I cringe inwardly, and probably outwardly too. I'm at a loss for a comeback.

I was naive to think he wouldn't read between the lines when I casually asked if Pearl was also a regular.

Such a backfired attempt!

I can only hope that everyone is too buried in their phones to notice me.

"Well, hope it works out for you," Randy continues with a low hum. "Good to see a young, popular man like you still chasing after love, just like we did back in the day."

"Ha ha, so you thought we were just skating by without any effort?"

"You know how it is, your fans are always raving about you guys, so I figured you just picked the prettiest one and called it a day," Randy says, his tone wistful. "Which would explain why marriage looks different now compared to our time."

"How is marriage different now?"

"People want a good marriage without any of the work."

"So, marriage is quite the challenge, huh?" I've never really pondered marriage before, but I can definitely see how tough it must be to constantly share your life with someone and never have your own space. I'm genuinely baffled by how people navigate it all.

"It's not that it's hard. Marriage isn't complicated, but in order to be happily married, two people have to put in the effort to understand each other, communicate openly, and grow together."

Randy's words sink in. I wonder if I'll ever find that special someone I'd be willing to spend the rest of my life with.

With that thought lingering, a bell rings, and when I turn my head, I see her—the one person who's unknowingly turned me into a stalker. Yet, all I want is a simple, normal conversation with her. She's wearing a dark brown floral dress, a cardigan draped over her shoulders, and her golden hair pulled back into a ponytail. Her eyes seem even brighter today, matching the gold necklace and earrings she has on.

Her eyes land on me and there's a flicker of panic in her expression before she swiftly averts her gaze and heads toward the door again. I hurriedly make my way over to her. "Hey, hey. You just got in?"

"What do you want, Zane? Why are you here again today?" Her tone is curt and her guard is up.

"Same as you. I told you Randy's coffee is the best. And, well, I was also hoping to run into you since you didn't give me your number."

"You have my work number. Call me during office hours or leave a message. Otherwise, this feels like harassment." Her words take the wind out of my sails.

Is she genuinely not interested in talking to me? I thought she was only putting up this front, but what if she really has no desire for a friendship with me?

I swallow my pride and decide to change tactics. I'm going to bend my rule of never resorting to coercion, just this once.

"I'm sorry. I didn't mean to bother you. I just really want someone I can talk to, you know? I'm going through so much, and Coach really talked you up," I say, the words leaving a bitter taste in my mouth. The only fib there is the idea of needing someone to confide in. Opening up to anyone about my problems is something I usually avoid. But desperate times call for desperate measures if I'm ever gonna get a shot with Pearl.

Her expression softens. "I promise I'm looking for the right person for you to talk to and process everything that's going on with you."

"I meant I need to talk to you as a friend," I say as sincerely as possible.

"Just a friend?" she asks skeptically.

"Yes, of course. Only as a friend."

"Are you sure?" She squints her eyes, trying to discern my expression beneath the cover of my hood and sunglasses.

"Your suspicious eyes tell me you don't quite buy it. Why's that?" I smirk.

She twiddles her fingers, her body swaying slightly from side to side. "I don't know, guys like you are never looking for friends. You already have enough of that on your team, I'd assume."

"How about I get you today's coffee and tell you how I'm not the guy you think I am?" I propose, guiding her back to the counter.

She gives me a once-over again, and I quickly add, "In a very friendly way."

Finally, she relaxes her shoulders, and I breathe a sigh of relief as I order our drinks, along with Randy's danish—which turns out to be one of her favorites too. Looks like we're off to a good start.

14

Pearl Davis

I can't believe I ended up here.

Sitting with Zane in the back corner of Randy's café was definitely not my brightest decision, especially after he removed his sunglasses and I realized the predicament I'd landed myself in.

His hood is still pulled over his head and he adjusted his chair to face me, making sure that he's angled toward the wall to avoid being spotted. And there's just a tiny table between us.

Everything about this interaction feels wrong.

I really don't want to be seen with a guy, especially in a corner of a café in a town where gossip spreads faster than wildfire. The last thing I need is rumors flying around about me being on a date and squandering all my chances of finding my soulmate.

No, I'm only here because Zane needs a friend, or at least that's what I keep telling myself every time I find myself getting lost in his eyes.

So far, he's been talking about his recent game, which I pretended to know nothing about, and the potential of becoming captain, but he admits he needs to bridge some gaps with his team, especially one guy he's been butting heads with since he joined the Glaciers.

I'm offering very little advice. I'm mostly just paddling in the ocean of his eyes, making sure not to drown.

He has this intense way of maintaining eye contact that's only unsettling because it's him. Meanwhile, I'm caught up analyzing the perfectly symmetrical lines of his jaw, almost too perfect to be natural. There have been plenty of awkward silences, which, in other circumstances, I'd fill with chatter, but I'm going to keep my distance and maintain the illusion that I never say much.

I need to be careful to avoid getting too attached. It's not my first rodeo with charming guys, and I know how it usually ends—with me being the one hurt.

Then there's the fact that he actually took my advice and is dressed in neutral colors today. It's a subtle detail, but our color palettes match so perfectly that I'm imagining how cute we'd look together in a picture.

It's a weird thought for someone who doesn't take pictures all that much, but I've always had a thing for color coordination and envisioning matching outfits for future family photos.

Uh oh, these musings are definitely not appropriate for a coffee hangout with Zane.

"You've been awfully quiet, considering how many people in your practice's reviews say you're quite the conversationalist," he says, taking another slow sip of his coffee.

He read the reviews on my practice? Heat creeps up my cheeks.

I definitely shouldn't blurt out the questions swirling in my mind, like why he's sporting a full tan in the middle of March. That's information I absolutely don't need to know.

"Well, talking to people is sort of my specialty, but I'm not exactly wearing my therapist hat today, am I?"

"So, does that mean you're not much of a talker when you're not on the clock?"

I bite my lip. I can't tell him the truth, but I also don't want to lie to him. He can't know that my silence is my self-protecting mechanism. I can't fathom being just friends with someone I clearly find this attractive and I'm weirdly so drawn to. Maybe some people can, but I know for a fact I'm not one of those people.

Before I can respond, I spot Kate and Duke approaching the café as I look through the window, and a sinking feeling settles in the pit of my stomach. I think they are coming inside Randy's because that's where I met Duke.

"You look stressed, like you're late for something?" Zane observes.

I scramble for an excuse. "I really have to go," I blurt out, hastily gathering my things.

"Can we do this again? Tomorrow maybe?" Zane suggests.

But I can't think about tomorrow right now. "I don't come to Randy's on Saturdays," I reply, trying to sound apologetic.

Zane doesn't miss a beat. "Great, that means I can take you somewhere different. Somewhere low-key?"

"Hmm, can we table that for now? Gotta go," I mutter, rushing toward the door without even thanking him for the coffee. I feel like a complete dupe, but the thought of facing Kate and Duke without Robyn by my side is enough to send me into a panic. And I definitely don't want them to see me with a guy like Zane and tell the whole church. I'm not sure he wants that either.

When I reach the door, they are already coming inside, holding hands with bright smiles on their faces. My muscles tense instinctively, but I force a smile.

"Pearl, hi!" Kate squeals.

"Hi," I reply, summoning every ounce of enthusiasm I can muster.

"I actually wanted to talk to you about the engagement party," Kate continues, her voice bubbling with excitement. "The girls want to do something after church. I said you'd obviously be there, but what about Robyn? Do you think she'll be available? Please beg her to come. It's super last minute, but I couldn't say no to them throwing us a party."

Out of genuine curiosity, I ask, "What made you so sure I don't have plans on Sunday evening?"

Kate bats her eyelashes. "Come on, Pearl. It's you."

I raise an eyebrow. "What does that mean?"

"Sorry if that came out wrong. But seriously, unless you have a date with Robyn, which I'd kindly ask you to reschedule, it's not like you do anything else outside work and church, do you? And, uhm, you don't date either."

I'm completely floored by her words. Nothing she said is untrue, but it's the way she says it and the fact that she says it at all that makes this the most awkward conversation I've ever had with Kate. And with Duke standing right next to her, I feel even more embarrassed.

"I'm sorry, I do have plans," I blurt out. But even as the words escape my lips, I feel the sorrowful tug of the Holy Spirit within me. Yet, the sinful part of me refuses to stand idly by as another woman snatches a man I once had a crush on and trample over me in the process.

"Come on, Pearl, are you lying to us? What plans could those be?" Kate presses.

Now I'm gulping, feeling as if all the air has been sucked out of my lungs. This is how it always starts, isn't it? One small lie leads to another until it spirals out of control. Why did I put myself in this situation? Why did I feel the need to defend my stupid honor? Who even cares if I don't date? It's not like Kate and Duke are the arbiters of my love life. I haven't found the right one yet, and that's more about God's timing than mine. So who am I even trying to please here? Certainly not myself, because now I'm about to admit I lied, and these two wouldn't care about my dating life if their lives depended on it.

I'm breaking into a cold sweat and suddenly I feel a presence behind me. Judging by Kate and Duke's startled expressions and the way their mouths are currently forming perfect *O*s, I know it's Zane behind me—I can even detect his distinct fresh smell.

My heart skips a beat as he speaks up. "With me. She has plans with me." I subtly turn to find him standing very close to me, his towering height making me tilt my head up to meet his gaze. The seriousness in his eyes ties knots in my stomach.

What's going on?

"Zane Ortiz, the legendary center?" Duke says, extending his hand.

"How?" Kate manages to utter, clearly taken aback.

I want to ask the same question, or maybe just faint. Fainting sounds like a tempting option right now, especially since Zane just risked being seen in public to save me from this embarrassing showdown.

"Can I take a picture with you? I've been raving about last night's game." Duke practically pushes me aside to ask for a selfie, and suddenly multiple people are lining up to take pictures with Zane. I'm left staring at the chaos, feeling responsible for it all.

Trusting my gut, I make a swift exit. I stride quickly to my office without saying a word to anyone.

I should have thanked Zane, but with him becoming a live photo booth, there was no telling when that spectacle was gonna end.

I enter my office and quickly reach for my next client's file, but my mind is still reeling from everything that's just happened. I can't shake off the question of why Zane would risk so much to save me from my own lies.

15

Zane Ortiz

Leaving Randy's café turned out to be a stroke of luck. I should've known that dropping by during lunchtime would come with a price, but I never imagined it would be this intense. It feels like I spent an eternity posing for pictures and signing autographs. By the time I finally pull into my garage, I'm utterly drained.

Don't get me wrong, I appreciate my fans and their support. But the whole smiling-for-the-camera routine? It's just not my thing. I'm more comfortable as the mysterious, brooding hockey player that's untouchable. And that reputation hasn't steered me wrong, even if it means people assume I'm easily angered. Although that seemed to be the case when I overheard that girl talking down to Pearl.

I couldn't help but listen in. I shouldn't have been eavesdropping, but I've got a thing for sniffing out tension. And after feeling powerless for so long, I can't stand by and watch someone else get bullied.

Maybe the girl didn't mean any harm, but from Pearl's voice, I could tell she wasn't having a good time being belittled about her weekend plans. I know it wasn't my place, but I had to step in.

What surprised me most was how quickly Pearl left without saying a word. I wonder if she didn't need me to intervene.

Did I make things worse? Did I ruin any chance of getting to know her?

There's only one way to find out. I pull up her practice's number and give her a call. After a few rings, she picks up.

"Hey, Sweet P," I greet her, fully aware that the new nickname gets under her skin. It's good to know that the only other person who calls her this isn't a Robert as I had feared. When I overheard the conversation earlier, they mentioned a Robyn, and she must definitely be Pearl's Robs.

Now I know for sure she's single and I have gained a few other insights into her —all the tidbits she didn't want to give me willingly.

"Hi, Zane? Why do you keep calling me that?"

"I like it. I mean, I thought it was pretty unique at first, but I don't mind sharing this with Robs."

"If you must know," she sighs, "Robyn only calls me P, and she's my best friend."

"Ahh, so there isn't a Robert?" I pretend to only figure it out now. "Then it's settled, Sweet P."

"Why did you call the office?" she asks dryly, sounding like she has no clue why I'm calling.

Hello, it's the huge elephant in the room.

I decide to play along. "Since you refused to give me your personal number, how else do you suggest I reach you?"

"Why do you need my phone number if you've already decided to always stalk me at Randy's?"

"I don't think I'm gonna step foot there for at least a couple of weeks." I can't risk another swarm of fans. They can't know that Randy's café is my spot.

There's no way today would be a repeat so soon.

"I'm sorry. That was all my fault. I just don't know why you felt the need to blow your cover for me."

"I didn't do it for you. I've been trying to make plans with you for a few days now, so when the opportunity arose, I had to take it." I joke.

In reality, I couldn't just sit back and watch. I guess it's a bit of a pet peeve of mine—seeing people being picked on, especially for something as trivial as not having a packed social calendar. If anything, Pearl and I are more alike than I thought.

"Something's seriously wrong with you, Zane. Did you take a puck to the head or something?"

"Oh, you're full of jokes," I respond, amused. "Look at that. This is the friendliest you've ever been with me. Are you one of those people who are lively on calls but turn into a total introvert in person?"

I hear a giggle at the end of the line, and it stirs something inside me.

"Again, I'm sorry. You seem like someone who prefers to keep a low profile. I can't imagine what it was like dealing with all those people."

"Don't sweat it, unless you're bailing on our Sunday plans. It's all part of the job, and I figured sooner or later I'd be caught at Randy's during the lunch rush," I chuckle, trying to downplay the chaos. I don't want her feeling guilty—it was my decision to be seen. "But seriously, why didn't you just say you weren't up for their engagement party? It was on such short notice. Anyone would've understood."

She pauses. "I couldn't. I'm not known for saying no to things."

"*Pfft*, you say no to me all the time. In fact, you love saying no. It's like declining invitations is your favorite thing to do."

"I mean, Kate and Duke are my friends from church. I feel so guilty I lied to them. I try not to lie. I'm a Christian."

"I guess it wasn't your finest Christian moment. But don't beat yourself up; technically, you didn't lie since you and I have plans on Sunday."

She shifts gears abruptly. "Are you a believer?"

"What does that have to do with our plans?"

"I stopped dating guys who don't share the same values as me a long time ago," she says curtly.

"Who said anything about a date? I told you I just need a friend, and I know you could be a good one." I, on the other hand, have no problem bending the truth as long as I'm not harming anyone and it helps me get to know her.

"I still don't understand your intentions with me, Zane. I know you're trying to hit on me, and the fact that you keep denying it makes you sus."

"Me? Suspicious? Never. If you don't want to rope me into your lie, then let's plan something for Sunday. Now, I need your number to coordinate."

I hear her growl in frustration, but she relents and gives me her number before bidding me goodbye.

Now that I have her number, I can bother her anytime.

I may have to thank Kate and Duke after all.

16

Pearl Davis

I slump back in my chair as my last client and his mom exit my office. Another successful session. It always warms my heart when foster parents are proactive about therapy. It not only helps the kids process their emotions but also strengthens the bond between them and their guardians.

It's a known fact that children in foster care who actively seek mental and emotional support, with the help of the system or their caregivers, are more likely to find a forever home.

I love my calling.

Sometimes, it's hard to believe that this is my job. A Christian therapist once saved me when I was just thirteen years old, angry at the world for never knowing my parents.

When Beatrice first suggested therapy, I was ready to put up a fight. No one had ever asked me how I felt in all the homes I had been shuffled through. But Beatrice and Fynn were different. They never had children, yet they cared

THE GAME SHE HATES 91

for me more than I ever imagined parents could. Without them, I might have aged out of the system and ended up on the streets, maybe with a child of my own. That's what happened to many of my childhood friends who didn't get the blessing I did—to be paired with a God-fearing couple who helped me untangle the mess of my young emotions with a professional therapist.

I continued seeing the same therapist regularly even in my early twenties. While I knew I had found complete healing when Jesus entered my heart, navigating early adulthood was a challenge, especially with Beatrice and Fynn no longer reachable as they had been called to serve the Lord in Cambodia. Our contact was limited to sporadic emails updating me on their missionary work. My therapist became the only other person who truly knew me and whom I could confide in—before I met Robyn. Most of our sessions in college revolved around my relationship struggles with guys.

I've always been the type of person who genuinely enjoys getting to know people, which has often landed me in unexpected relationships with a lot of guys. Unfortunately, those relationships never seemed to last. Either I compromised my values to date unbelievers, or I fell for guys who pretended to share my faith in Jesus only to reveal their true intentions later on—that was Clay, two years ago.

My past experiences have taught me all I need to know about guys like Zane. I believe God has someone special for me; He's promised me a family, and even at twenty-eight and single, I still hold onto that hope. In the meantime, I just need to get better at dodging the wrong guys.

It doesn't help that I have a tendency to fall for someone in a heartbeat, and making plans with Zane this Sunday feels like the wrong move for a girl like me.

I glance at my watch. It's time to go home. Robyn and I have a girl's night planned every Friday.

I tidy up my desk and organize the files, making sure the file on top is the one for my first appointment on Monday. My organizational skills are always at play. Everything has its place, and I thrive on systems and routines.

I turn off the lights and adjust the thermostat to a slightly chillier setting. It's not the warmest March, but there's no need to crank up the heat and risk a high utility bill.

·♥·♥·♥·♥·♥·

Robyn and I are treating ourselves to our favorite dishes at *Fiesta Grill*. I got my usual enchiladas with two sides of rice and black beans, topped with my favorite toppings. Robyn, on the other hand, switches it up between quesadillas, tostadas, and chalupas. Today she went for the chalupa with the same sides as mine, but her toppings are a bit spicier than mine. I prefer to keep it on the milder side.

The queso at *Fiesta Grill* is incredible—the kind that seems designed to spoil your appetite. We always end up taking some home because they serve so much! We love using it later with chips at home, although our chips aren't quite as perfectly salted as the ones here.

"So, why are you keeping me waiting? I'm dying to hear what happened at the cafe," Robyn prods eagerly, taking a bite of her food.

"First of all, I need you to be my best friend and not Zane's fan when I tell you this."

"I've always been both, but I'll try," she says, putting on a serious face.

I can only hope Robyn sees the danger in all this and brings me back to my senses instead of fangirling about some hockey player and our supposed friendship.

"We met again at Randy's today, although this time he didn't make it sound like it was an accident. He apparently wanted to run into me."

"What? He said that?" She starts screaming and fanning herself with a napkin.

"Robs, focus, we already talked about this. I've been burned too many times with worldly guys. I can't let Zane even be an option in my mind."

"True, you've been in an awful lot of bad relationships." She takes another bite of her chalupa.

Not the reminder I needed right now, but at least she's focused.

"Right. So he mentioned needing someone to talk to, and you know how I am. I've seen how not having anyone to talk to can lead to depression first-hand. We sat for coffee, and he opened up about a few hockey-related issues he's dealing with."

"*Ugh*, lucky you," she interrupts, slamming her hand on the table hard enough to make the water in her glass ripple. "I would have loved to be at that table. His last game ended with him in the penalty box again," she adds with a touch of sadness in her tone.

I purposefully didn't tell Robyn that I had watched the game at Kate's, mainly because I was only interested in catching glimpses of Zane whenever the camera was on him. The last thing I want is for her to insist on going to a game with me in person.

I'd be caught red-handed, and I've kept my attraction to him a secret from her. It's information I've deemed irrelevant.

"Not where I'm going with this." I give her a glare.

"Okay." She beckons with her hand, urging me to spill it already.

"So I saw Duke and Kate coming to the café from where we were sitting, and I tried to make a quick escape, but Zane delayed me, asking if we could get together again. I really don't remember what I told him because I was panicking. I can't explain why seeing Kate with Duke still makes me feel weird. I know I no longer have a crush on Duke, but I just didn't want to be seen with a guy. You know how rumors can be. Anyway, I couldn't exit in time, and we got to the door at the same time. Kate was happy to see me, and when she invited me to her engagement party on Sunday, I lied about having plans."

"Why did you lie? You hate lies." Robs' eyes widen with concern.

"I know God does too. I'm not proud of it. But that's not all." I skip the part where Kate belittled me about never having plans. Robyn is intense and can't stand anyone being mean to me; that would be the thread that breaks the camel's back in her already-distant relationship with Kate.

"Go on."

"So when I lied, she obviously didn't believe me. It's no secret I don't have much of a life outside work, church, and, well, you. Then Zane came up behind me and blurted out that we had plans together on Sunday."

"Wait, he was listening to your conversation?"

"You know Kate's voice. She doesn't need a mic to be heard. But I had no idea he was eavesdropping too."

"How did I miss this epic movie?" She runs her hand across her face.

"It was embarrassing at best," I say, rolling my eyes.

"But he saved you, didn't he?"

"He did, but now he wants us to follow through with the Sunday plans."

She smirks. "It'd be two lies if you didn't."

"Ugh, he said the same exact thing. But do you really think I should go out with Zane? I mean, me, Pearl Davis, the girl you've labeled as being boy crazy," I say pointing both index fingers to myself.

"It doesn't have to look like a date," she says, and I furrow my brows, not understanding her point. "I won't say no to tagging along if you ask nicely." She shrugs.

My heart races. Why didn't I think of this? "Are you serious? Would you come with me? I really need you to make sure I don't get attached to him," I say, biting the inside of my cheek to suppress any words that might reveal my growing attraction to him.

"Girl, yeah! I have so many questions about this season. I'd love to come. Just make sure you ask him first. Despite him being in your face all the time, he is a celebrity and needs privacy."

She's right. I really don't see Zane as a celebrity. He's not exactly subtle for someone supposedly famous. I mean, stalking someone like me in a coffee shop?

He also doesn't know how to blend in. If it wasn't for my advice, he'd probably show up next time wearing neon colors. That thought makes me smile. I'm glad Robyn's looking down at her phone.

"I'll ask him."

"You have his number too?" she asks, surprised.

"No, he took mine to coordinate," I say, swatting her for looking at me suspiciously.

"You are living so many girls' dreams and you don't even know it."

"Robs, is this your dream? Do you want to date Zane?" I know Robyn doesn't date, but what if all this is rubbing in her face something she'd want for herself? I'd hate for it to be the case, and I'd do anything to cut off Zane for this reason.

"Relax. I don't date, and I absolutely would not date someone I'm a huge fan of. So trust me, I'm only saying that because I am on social media and I see how girls rave about Zane Ortiz."

I sigh in relief, unsure if it's because I'm glad I don't have to cut off Zane immediately—though I know I'll still need to if I want to avoid another disappointment or, worse, getting hurt.

17

Zane Ortiz

"I can't believe you thought P was a fan," Robyn says, laughing and sipping on her mocktail.

This lunch turned out to be more enjoyable than I expected. When Pearl mentioned that her roommate would join us, I welcomed Robyn's company without any hesitation. I wasn't about to risk anything that might distance me from Sweet P.

From the moment I laid my eyes on her, I felt an inexplicable pull, as if she belonged in my life. I am open to endure whatever antics or obstacles as long as it means getting to know her.

Except Robyn is an absolute joy to be around. She's a hardcore Glaciers fan and really into hockey. Despite not playing it herself, she possesses incredible insights and noteworthy strategies for our team. Robyn has attended all our local games and can recite each recent match with impressive detail. She knows every player's strengths and weaknesses and discusses game tactics like a seasoned coach. It's clear that she's studied each player carefully, and that's the kind of fan I'd love to hang out with—someone who genuinely appreciates everything about the game.

I'm conscious of not getting too caught up. I don't want Pearl to feel left out. It almost feels as though Pearl brought Robyn along to divert my attention, but it would take more than a hockey enthusiast to draw my gaze away from her.

They are both sitting across from me at *La Basilique*, a charming French restaurant I originally booked when it was just meant to be Pearl and me. Soft, ambient lighting bathes the space in a warm, inviting glow, while smooth jazz melodies fill the air.

Although my seat doesn't offer a view outside, I can't complain too much about the sight in front of me. Pearl looks stunning in a mustard maxi dress with thin straps, her hair styled in an elegant updo.

She must be one of those people who always dress in their Sunday best. I love that her style is never flashy, but always elegant and classy in her own way.

"I just don't get how someone can hate hockey," I say, pulling Pearl into the conversation.

"Hate may be a strong word. I just don't care for the game," she replies.

"You have no basis to say that when you haven't even come to a game," I tease, raising an eyebrow.

"I wouldn't even know what's going on." She gives me her adorable shy smile.

What a beauty!

"She's never even watched a game on TV. I'm telling you, she can't stand hockey. I think it's the fights," Robyn interjects.

Pearl looks a bit embarrassed. I hope I didn't make her feel less for not being interested in my favorite sport. I know it's not for everyone, even though this little town makes it seem like it is.

I decide to change the subject. "So, what do you like to do for fun? How do you relax?"

"I like to read," Pearl responds, her eyes sparkling with enthusiasm. Clearly, she doesn't need to share my passion for hockey. She has her own thing.

"What do you read?" I notice Robyn checking her phone, giving us some space to chat.

"I read it all. Fiction, nonfiction, textbooks," Pearl answers with a laugh.

"I think the last time I read was in high school for homework," I admit, expecting her to poke fun at me.

"Reading is a great escape for me. It's like traveling without spending a dime. But I guess you already travel a lot for games and stuff."

"Yeah, we do travel, but it's nothing like going on a vacation. We're only there for the game."

Her phone rings, and Pearl looks at me apologetically. It's the first time her phone has interrupted our conversation, and I don't mind her taking the call. It's probably important. I nod at her, signaling that she should answer.

Before she picks up, Pearl glances at Robyn, showing her the caller ID. Robyn's expression changes, and I can tell they both recognize the significance of this interruption.

Sensing that they might need a moment to talk privately, I decide to give them some space. "Excuse me," I say with a slight smile. "I'll use the restroom real quick."

I walk around the corner toward the restroom area, following the hallway that seems to lead toward the kitchen. The air is filled with the delightful scents of fine wine and freshly baked bread. Elegant chandeliers cast a soft light overhead, and I catch a glimpse of a vintage clock hanging on the wall, its hands ticking away steadily.

I stand by the restroom entrance and keep glancing at the clock.

Several *restroom acceptable* minutes pass and I'm about to peek around the corner to see if Pearl is done, when I inadvertently overhear Robyn's voice echoing from our table.

I pause, caught between the desire not to eavesdrop and my genuine curiosity about Pearl's difficulty in saying no to certain people—something she hasn't struggled with when it comes to me.

"You have got to learn to say no sometimes, P. If you don't want to be there, why force yourself, especially if they told you at the last minute?"

"How are you encouraging this? You're the one who urged me to go back to church and stop wallowing in my pain," Pearl's voice echoes. "And Lydia thinks it looks bad that two bridesmaids are missing."

"But you're over Duke, aren't you? It's not the same as missing church because you were heartbroken. We're out and having a good time with our friend, Zane Ortiz."

"You just met him. We've known Kate for years, and we're bridesmaids."

My heart sinks at the mention of Duke and a broken heart. Frozen in place, I wrestle with the dilemma of having overheard something I shouldn't have. Should I let them see me and let Pearl wonder if I heard about Duke breaking her heart? Or should I stay hidden, count to ten, and then return?

Deciding to stay put, I take a deep breath and quietly count to regain composure. After a moment, I turn and make my way back toward our table.

I clear my throat lightly to signal my return. The air around the table feels charged with the weight of what I had overheard, and I struggle to find the right words to break the tension.

"Everything okay?" I ask.

Pearl looks up, her expression full of concern. Robyn's gaze meets mine briefly before she shifts her focus back to Pearl.

"You remember the couple that invited me to their engagement party?" Pearl begins, her tone slightly hesitant.

"Of course. That's kind of hard to forget," I reply, carefully avoiding mentioning Kate's and Duke's names after overhearing their conversation.

"Robyn and I are bridesmaids, and another bridesmaid called us asking us to come to the party for a few minutes. And, honestly, she has a point. We should be there."

"So, I take it you and the bride are close?" I ask.

Robyn shakes her head immediately, but Pearl nods. "We've been attending the same church for a while. We've done small groups together and led the youth. I wouldn't call her a best friend, but we're definitely friends."

"Of course you wouldn't. That seat is already taken," Robyn says with a mischievous smirk, pointing to herself.

The smile Pearl gives Robyn is one for the books. I can only hope to receive such a genuine smile from her someday.

"I can come with you if you want. It's my recovery day," I offer.

Pearl furrows her brow in confusion. "Why would you subject yourself to another fan attack?"

"As long as you don't leave me this time, I won't mind." A grin forms on her perfect lips.

"I think that's perfect. The whole church is filled with Glaciers fans. It might be a bit awkward at first, but they'll warm up to you and treat you like one of their own after a while," Robyn says with much enthusiasm.

"Well, I don't know about the single ladies who're ready to mingle, treating you normally, but I'm sure you're used to girls flirting with you," Pearl adds.

The way she says it, it's almost like she's daring me to back out. I'm definitely used to women flirting with me, but lately, I haven't been responding to any of them. With my mind solely focused on Pearl, I doubt anyone will succeed in diverting my attention from her, especially now that I know Duke broke her heart. My reason for going is none other than to ensure he doesn't have the opportunity to hurt her again.

18

Zane Ortiz

I haven't been to many engagement parties, but none have ever taken place in a church. Duke and Kate's celebration is in the church hall, which I gather is the same church Coach and Pearl attend. Thankfully, Coach isn't here tonight; otherwise, he'd definitely wonder why I'm crashing this shindig.

The evening kicked off with a flurry of everyone inviting me to take selfies with them. It was amusing to see their surprised expressions when I arrived with Pearl and Robyn, which conveniently excused their tardiness. Kate even remarked that she understood why Pearl had initially declined the invitation, saying, "It's not every day one gets to hang out with Zane Ortiz. Thanks for bringing him here."

After a while, people resumed mingling with each other, and I was relieved to no longer be the center of everyone's attention. However, a few persistent bridesmaids continue to cast curious glances my way. I've been strategically distancing myself from them all night.

I'm not exactly a party guy, but I do appreciate this ambiance—the soft music, the relaxed chatter that doesn't drown out conversation like it does in bars. And I'm grateful for the absence of alcohol. Booze is a big no-go for me; it's a trigger. A reminder of what it used to do to my dad and the pain I endured at his hands.

In a few weeks, April will be here, and the man will be released from prison.

I've been trying to push these thoughts aside ever since Aunt Melissa brought it up. Sometimes I pretend I've forgotten what he looks like, but it's difficult when we share so many features. No one had to tell me; growing up, I could see how I was a version of him, and I hated it. But after breaking free from his influence, the only reminders of him are bullies and alcohol.

I'm standing with Duke and a few other guys he introduced me to, though their names have already slipped my mind. Meanwhile, Robyn and Pearl are catching up with their girlfriends and taking pictures near the photo booth.

From where I'm standing, I can discreetly keep my eyes on Pearl. I'm trying not to make it too obvious, but I've never encountered anyone quite like her. If kindness had a face, it would look like hers.

I'm still not sure why I have all these profound thoughts and feelings about her; she's made it challenging for me to break through her walls. Nevertheless, I'm determined to keep trying when I get a chance this evening.

Duke notices me gazing in a particular direction and follows my line of sight. I can't imagine he knows which woman has captured my attention, but his presence brings to mind the hurt I heard in Pearl's voice when she mentioned him.

"So, how do you know Pearl and Robyn?" Duke asks casually.

"Just through Coach. I met Pearl first, and she introduced me to Robyn today," I reply, choosing not to disclose that we actually met during therapy at her practice.

"Ah, that makes sense," Duke says, his expression hinting at something more.

"What does?"

"Pearl hates hockey. So it makes sense you didn't meet at a game," Duke remarks, almost as if he finds it unfortunate.

I let out a snort. "It's what makes her unique." Everyone in this town only sees me as a pro athlete, but I appreciate how unimpressed Pearl is by that aspect of my life.

Duke then decides to offer me unsolicited advice about Pearl. "Just be careful. Take it from a guy she was into. She can be clingy, so approach your friendship with that in mind."

His comment strikes a nerve, and I fully turn to face him, my jaw clenched and nostrils slightly flared in irritation. "Glad she finally realized you two weren't a good fit," I say firmly, making it clear that he can't speak negatively about Pearl in my presence.

"Oh no," Duke counters confidently, "she never had the guts to tell me how she felt. I had a feeling about it, and when Kate and I started talking, she avoided us entirely, which only confirmed my suspicion. She gave off the vibe of an insecure woman, not a go-getter. I would have faded into the background if I dated her. It just wasn't attractive to me."

I can't believe Duke's words. How could anyone see Pearl differently from how I see her? Frustration brews inside me, but I choose to remain silent. He doesn't deserve my take on Sweet P.

I start walking away from him, heading toward the photo booth where Pearl is.

Pearl was.

Where is she? She can't possibly be gone.

Not again.

I pass by the group of girls still taking pictures and videos and they try to stop me, eager to include me. But I'm not in the mood after Duke's comments and not knowing where Pearl is.

Robyn approaches and informs me in a whisper, "She went outside."

I nod in thanks and relief and head toward the exit door.

19

Pearl Davis

I'm standing alone under the chilly night sky. I'm more captivated by the stars than by the idea of another camera flash blinding me. Don't get me wrong, I don't mind taking a few pictures, but after a handful of decent shots, my motivation tends to dwindle. Maybe it's because I don't have any social media accounts to share them on.

The only destination for my photos is a single picture attached to the occasional email to Beatrice and Fynn.

I wrap my arms around myself, wishing I had brought a cardigan. Then again, I hadn't planned anything else after the late lunch with Zane. I'm so glad Robyn tagged along; I don't think I could handle being alone with Zane. His gaze threatens to enthrall me, and his smile leaves me breathless. The genuine interest he shows in me only adds to my discomfort around him. I'm just a girl in search of her soulmate—I don't need this bait-and-switch in my life. I need to push him out somehow.

A voice interrupts my thoughts, and I instinctively jerk, turning to see Zane approaching.

Not him and me. Outside. Together. Alone.

"Sweet P, isn't it too cold to be out here?" he asks me while closing the distance between us.

"I just needed some air," I reply curtly, trying to steady my racing heart. Why does he have to be caring too.

"Are you sure you're fine?" He removes his jacket and drapes it over my shoulders. I slip my arms into the sleeves and feel myself engulfed in his intoxicating scent of spices and citrus. I wish I could bottle it up to keep it close forever.

When I meet his gaze, I see genuine concern impressed across his features.

"Yeah. Why do you ask?"

"It's just..." he pauses, exhaling slowly. "I accidentally overheard you and Robyn at the restaurant, mentioning Duke breaking your heart. I just want to make sure being here and celebrating him and Kate isn't too hard on you."

The dimness of the outside lights prevents me from getting lost in Zane's eyes, but I can still see him clearly enough to read the sincerity in his gaze.

Despite being here, I haven't thought about Duke at all. I can happily confirm I've finally moved on. "I'm really over it. We never dated or anything. I just had a big crush on him."

"Good to know. You deserve better than Duke."

I frown. "You don't even know the guy or me. What makes you say that?"

"The few words we spoke today told me everything I need to know about him. And about you," he says, his lopsided grin a delightful ache. "I've picked up on more than you realize about you."

"Can I ask you a question?"

"Shoot."

"Are you always eavesdropping?"

His serious expression softens into a smile.

"This is the second time you've done it. I just need to know if it's a recurring habit of yours."

"Ha ha, honestly, I've never been one to pry into others' affairs. But the way I grew up made me someone who is always hyper-aware of my surroundings. That includes picking up on conversations I probably shouldn't be privy to."

"How did you grow up?" I know it's a loaded question, one that would be fine in my professional setting. But with Zane, I shouldn't be asking this. I should be showing him the exit door out of my life.

"My mom died giving birth to me, and my dad is an alcoholic who has spent the last ten years in jail. He'll be released next month. You can imagine how it was growing up in those circumstances," Zane shares, surprising me with his candor. My heart aches with every word he just said.

His expression mirrors the surprise I feel. Was he also not planning to share this much?

At least *I* didn't know my parents. I knew they had given me up and were probably addicts of one kind or another. But Zane's story... A fat tear rolls down my cheek, and when he reaches to wipe it away, a shockwave of tingling travels down my neck, causing a shiver to ripple through my core.

"I'm sorry. I actually have no idea why I just told you all that. I never talk about it." He turns away, and I have to fight the urge not to gently turn his face back toward me. I want him to know how deeply sorry I am for what he went through, and if there's any way I may have inadvertently triggered painful memories for him, I hope he can find it in his heart to forgive me.

"Don't be sorry. Talking about your pain is good. I just...I know it's not fair to judge a book by its cover, but this...I couldn't have imagined. I'm really sorry to hear that."

He turns his face toward me again, his expression now devoid of any discernible emotion.

"It's fine. Life can be cruel. So what about you? Let me guess. Had a great childhood? Grew up in a home with loving parents and boundless joy?"

"Why is that your guess?"

"The way you carry yourself. You're kind, and it's like you can't frown. Even when you do, it's another one of your adorable expressions. And you care about people. That's why I call you Sweet P," he says, and at the mention of "adorable expressions" and the nickname he gave me, my heart quickens.

I do my best to consider everyone, but I wonder how he's been able to see that in me, especially when I've been trying to keep my distance from him.

"We can't do this, Zane."

"What?" he says, suddenly alarmed. "What can't we do?"

"This," I say, gesturing between us with my hand, "I'm not the girl for you."

He blesses me with his blinding smile, clearly playing the fool. "We're just having a conversation. As friends. Remember?"

"You really expect me to buy into the 'just friends' act?" I ask, crossing my arms over my chest. The gesture sends another gentle drift of his jacket's scent around me, reminding me that I'm wearing it. Why does he have to smell so irresistible?

"Why not?"

"This is why not," I say, pointing directly at his eyes. "Friends don't give me that look."

"You have a problem with my eyes?"

"It's the way you look at me. That's not the same look you gave Robyn or anyone else here."

He lifts his arms up in surrender. "I have no idea what you are talking about. I really want to get to know you. You seem different. I love that it doesn't have to be about hockey between us."

"I don't believe that's it. You've been looking at me like this since you spotted me the first time at Randy's before our appointment," I huff.

"Okay, you got me," he admits with a sheepish look. "You're beautiful. You caught my eye. I had no idea you were my therapist the first time I saw you at Randy's. And when I finally got in your office, I thought you were looking at me the same exact way. I even thought you were a fan because of how flustered you seemed. It made me want to talk and see where it goes. But you've made it clear since then that you don't want to explore the idea of us in a romantic capacity. But I still want you in my life. In any capacity. Except, obviously, as my therapist, because you'd never let me get close to you."

His words, his smile, his gaze, his honesty—everything about him leaves me speechless. My heart races with a pace I can't calm. How does someone as beautiful as him see any beauty in me?

"I never knew my parents," I start, and notice his eyebrows shoot up in surprise. "I grew up in the foster care system. I wasn't always kind. I was a kid who was mad at the world. I was rehomed too many times until, at thirteen, I landed in the home of angels.

"A couple named Beatrice and Fynn took me in. They introduced me to the gospel of Jesus Christ through the way they lived and loved. They cared for me until I left for college, and then they went to Asia for missionary work."

He inches closer.

What's he going to do? God, please, not this. I don't know if I have the self-control needed to resist kissing him back.

Instead, he takes me into his arms and squeezes me gently, my head resting against his broad chest. His heartbeat has a rhythmic sound, and I feel like melting into this hug. The way he holds me makes me wonder why he feels for me. He's clearly had it much worse.

He releases me, and I clear my throat before taking a few steps back. After the moment we just shared, I could definitely use some distance.

"I am so sorry for my assumption. I can't believe you went through that." His hand reaches for mine.

"Don't be. Jesus turned my worst experiences into something so beautiful."

"What are you talking about? What's beautiful about parents leaving their own child for the government to raise?"

"My days of questioning my biological parents are behind me. My experiences helped me to see my need for Jesus. I had no sense of identity and felt like I didn't belong to anyone. Discovering that God adopted me through Jesus Christ healed my wounded heart. Now, what I've been through enables me to empathize deeply with the children I counsel. I know how I can pray for them even when they aren't communicating well with me. I can easily approach them without judgment for their negative emotions and feelings because I've been there. My personal journey allows me to connect with them on a level that I wouldn't have achieved otherwise."

"I knew you were special," he murmurs, almost to himself.

"What's special is Jesus in me. Without him, I'm broken. We all are."

He purses his lips. "I've never thought about religion that way."

"It's not religion I'm talking about. What Jesus died for on the cross wasn't for me to adhere to a religious system. It was for me to have a personal relationship with God through Christ. That was the purpose of his ultimate sacrifice."

He shrugs and says, "I don't even know what that means."

"I didn't either. But if you're curious about what it means and how it could change your life, come to church next Sunday. We aren't a large congregation; it's mostly people you saw here today along with a few elderly people. I'll even help you find a low-key seat and I'll give you a signal at the end of the meeting so you can slip out before everyone else."

"You'd do that for me?" Zane asks, running his hands through his wavy hair.

It's a good question. The last time I invited a guy to church, my feelings were involved and things went sour.

If Zane also comes and finds his future wife in my church, I may never recover from this one.

"On second thought, we actually have an online service. I can send you the details."

"All right, sure. Thanks," he replies, with a mix of confusion and disappointment.

I take a deep breath. That was as close as I'll come to repeating my *Duke mistake*.

Gesturing for Zane to head back inside, I hand him his jacket.

People have definitely noticed our absence. Not that they'd have noticed me missing, but everyone knows Zane is here, so they're likely on the lookout for him and whoever he's with.

20

Zane Ortiz

It's been a whirlwind of a week—practice sessions, a tough game, and a string of brand deals lined up by my agent have kept me busier than ever. Despite my best efforts, I couldn't carve out a moment to see Pearl. Twice I attempted to coax her into joining me for dinner at my place, only to be met with polite refusals. She insisted that such invitations were beyond the bounds of friendship.

Our phone conversations have been a lifeline for me each evening. It became a ritual—I'd dial her number first, my heart pounding with anticipation until she picked up. Each time she answered, it made me second-guess her supposed resolve to keep our relationship strictly platonic.

The fact that each call lasted over two hours proved she was comfortable with me, and there also wasn't anything I felt I couldn't tell her. We dug into our pasts, and despite our hard upbringing, Pearl managed to unearth childhood moments that had us both in stitches. Leave it to her to resurrect some fond memories from my early years. I never knew I had those; my mind had been fixated on the darkest chapters for as long as I can remember. Our conversations lightly grazed past relationships a few times; she seemed hesitant to share those, hinting at wounds still fresh. It was clear someone, who wasn't even Duke, hadn't treated her as the gem she truly was, and all I wanted was to reassure her that she was worth more than the world's treasures.

The urge to pour my heart out is strong each time, but the thought of risking the easy rhythm we have—the very friendship that gives me the excuse to dial her number every night—keeps me silent. She isn't ready to hear the depth of my feelings just yet.

Pearl has a knack for listening to me and always knows just the right words to say, even if those words often came straight from her Bible. Her gentle reminders of God's unconditional love and His desire for my well-being stayed with me long after we hung up. I never imagined I'd start pondering faith and what it would truly mean if God did have a plan for me, and genuinely wanted what was best for me. Her words sparked a curiosity about the fulfillment found in wholeheartedly following Jesus.

As I dress in what I hope passes for suitable church attire—black jeans and a button-down—I can't help but wonder why she withdrew her invitation for me to attend in person and insisted I watch the sermon online.

How could she not want to see me as much as I wanted to see her?

I can't wait for Randy's café to stop buzzing with gossip about my unexpected appearance. It's crazy to hear that people and the paparazzi are still flocking there in hopes of seeing me.

The downsides of living in a small town!

Hopefully, by next week, they'll have moved on, and I can swing by to see if I can return to my routine of catching glimpses of Pearl every day.

I glance at my watch, feeling my heart hammer. If I don't get going, I might be late. But if I'm being honest, it's not the prospect of attending church that has my heart racing—it's the chance to see Pearl again. She has no idea I'll be joining her today, but I plan to give her a call on my way there. I can't risk her missing out on the service just because I'll be coming.

·♥·♥·♥·♥·♥·

"Hey, good morning," I greet through the car's speaker.

"Hi, any issues logging into the service?" she asks.

"No, everything's smooth sailing. I was wondering if you could do me a favor and secure that low-key seat we talked about."

"What? You're here?" Her voice carries a hint of surprise, maybe even happiness.

"Yes, I'm in the parking lot. Red sports car."

"You are just *full* of surprises. Okay. I'll be right out." The call ends, and moments later, Pearl, dressed in a peach ruffle dress, heads my way. I take a moment to admire her before stepping out of the car.

She is even more beautiful than I remember.

The wind tousles her curled hair, and though she's trying to maintain a serious expression, I can tell she's fighting back a smile. It reassures me that this surprise isn't unwelcome.

She approaches and I get out to greet her with a side hug which is appropriate for being at church. Besides, the last time I held her in my arms at the engagement party, she gladly pulled away and created distance between us as if I'd committed a faux pas.

In the few seconds of closeness, her fruity scent and the hint of vanilla in her hair envelop me.

Her eyes, a lighter shade of green in the sunlight, reflect my own image back at me. Her face still spellbinds me like nothing else I've seen before.

"I'll interpret that smile as a sign of a well-executed surprise, then?" I venture in a low voice, noticing the blush that tints her cheeks.

"Why didn't you tell me you were planning to come?" she asks, her gaze meeting mine.

"You withdrew your invitation, so I assumed you might try to dissuade me or even skip church yourself."

A smile tugs at her beautiful lips, but she quickly suppresses it. "I did no such thing. I'd never miss church to avoid you," she dismisses with a huff.

"So you agree you were avoiding me? I knew it," I tease, lifting one finger in mock accusation. "Care to explain?"

"You're going to miss out on the best part of the service." She quickly grabs my arm and pulls me along to start walking.

We are not holding hands but she still has her arm on my forearm. It takes everything inside me not to touch the small of her back as we walk.

This isn't the same Pearl I was with a week ago. She could never have been this friendly with me before. I realize our evening phone calls have had a greater impact than I initially thought. She's slowly allowing me into her circle.

Pearl ushers me inside and she directs me to sit between her and Robyn.

Robyn grins briefly when she sees me, then turns her attention back to the stage, singing along. I half-expected her to engage in some small talk, maybe about last week's game where I saw her in the VIP section. I had given her a ticket to enjoy the game up close, and she hadn't stopped thanking me since. Apparently, Coach usually hooked her up with decent seats, but never in the VIP section. I was glad I could do something nice for at least one of them. However, here in church, it's clear that Robyn isn't just a hockey fan; she's also a Christian, like Pearl, who enjoys attending church.

The quaint little church, a far cry from the large ones of my childhood with Aunt Melissa, instantly puts me at ease. The soft, dim lighting creates an intimate atmosphere that makes me feel like I might blend into the background for the entire service. Especially since we're seated in what seems to be the *elderly aisle*—everyone back here is at least sixty-five.

This must have been Pearl's idea of a low-key spot. She is so thoughtful.

I wonder if Pearl and Robyn chose this section to accommodate me. Maybe they even passed up sitting with their friends to keep things discreet. It's hard to miss that the middle and front left rows are where all the young people are sitting.

After the worship service, Kate joins Duke in the front row. Their not-so-subtle display of affection—a quick kiss before she settles beside him—doesn't go unnoticed.

I don't know everything about Pearl but it's clear to me that Duke and she could never have been a good fit.

His words echo in my mind: *"I would have faded into the background if I dated her."* The sting of those words still bothers me.

Duke could never appreciate Pearl the way I do—the little things, like her desire to remain unseen and her contentment with being different. It's something I admire and even long for myself, especially the deep sense of contentment despite everything she's been through.

I've never paid much attention in church before, but the preacher's words are surprisingly easy to follow. Everything he says is accompanied by a Bible verse, which Pearl diligently notes down in her journal. She hasn't glanced my way since the sermon began, and neither has Robyn. They are both so focused and intent.

Pearl's arm keeps brushing against mine, and with each touch, a subtle flutter stirs within me. I doubt she even notices how often it's happening. Probably not, but these little moments are making this whole church experience even more enjoyable than it already unexpectedly is.

After a truly intriguing message about Jesus and how even his closest disciples often misunderstood his earthly mission—to exemplify living in accordance with God's will and demonstrate what a profound connection to the Father looks like—I'm left with even more questions and a desire for more.

I'm still sorting through what I just heard when communion begins.

Pearl leans in close and her delicious fruity scent wafts into my nostrils, and she whispers to me, "We have communion every Sunday, but it's not a ritual. It's a meaningful way for believers in Jesus Christ to remember his sacrifice for our sins."

I sigh in relief, grateful that Pearl didn't judge me for not going forward—though judgment isn't something I've ever received from her, not even for a second. Still, I'm glad she stopped me.

Communion must be a really special thing for Christians then. I make a mental note to add communion to the list of questions I have. Maybe Tyler would be willing and able to answer all these. He's been dying to talk to me in his Christian language without me cutting him off for years now. I can't wait to see his reaction when I approach him with all this.

After communion ends, Pearl signals for me to slip out before the service concludes. I realize I had a skewed view of church; I thought coming here would feel like hanging out, but we barely had a chance to talk. Now, all I want is more time with her.

I turn to Robyn, knowing she could help me convince Pearl, and ask, "If you're free, how about coming over for lunch at my place? Both you and Pearl, please."

"You know you really just want to invite Pearl. Why not just ask her to come along with you?"

"You've got me there," I admit with a chuckle. "But she won't come if you're not with her. Plus, I can see us becoming friends too. What do you say?"

I can really see myself being friends with someone as down-to-earth as Robyn. She shows signs of rooting for Pearl and me, but in a very subtle way, probably because she doesn't want to upset her friend.

"All right. Want a piece of advice?"

"Please!"

"She needs to trust you. She needs to know that your intentions are pure and align with her values." Robyn may be my biggest fan when I'm on the ice but she could not be more loyal to her best friend. I respect that about her.

"Got it. You're the best," I say gratefully and turn to Pearl as she rises for another song. Leaning close, I whisper, "Lunch at my place. Robyn is coming," and swiftly walk toward the exit, not giving her a chance to refuse.

It's just a friendly lunch at my house.

21

Pearl Davis

Zane's house towers proudly in a nice neighborhood. Inside, it's like stepping into a catalog spread—everything's shiny and new. The ceilings are so high, and there's this big open space between the kitchen and the living room. The tile floors sparkle and guide us past some seriously comfy-looking brown leather sofas, with a big TV mounted above the fireplace, practically begging for a movie night with popcorn.

The staircase curves, leading to the upper floor. This isn't what I pictured when I imagined his house, *not that I spent much time thinking about it*. For someone who's always on the road and spends a lot of time practicing, I didn't expect his house to be so well-coordinated. Despite its impeccable organization, there's a distinct lack of personal touch. There are no photos, no knick-knacks—just a few paintings that look like they could've come straight from a gallery. I wonder if he's the one who painted them.

He did mention painting and drawing during the off season.

Robyn and I share a glance, both feeling a bit like fish out of water as we take in the spectacle. Zane, leaning casually against the sleek kitchen island, watches us with that trademark smirk of his. The kitchen itself is a chef's dream, with walnut-colored cupboards and shiny new appliances, including what looks like the biggest stove I've ever seen. Guy must really love to cook.

"You can both say it. It's too big of a house for one person. I know it too," Zane remarks, running a hand through his hair—a habit he seems to have when he's not sure what to do with himself. It's cute.

"You live here all by yourself? No roomie, no pets?" Robyn asks, her eyes wide with disbelief.

Zane nods, that smirk of his growing even wider. "Just me."

Robyn gives me the side-eye, probably wondering why I didn't want to come here with her after Zane pulled a fast one by inviting her instead of me, knowing she'd jump at the chance to hang out with him.

She's living the dream, getting to chill at the abode of her favorite hockey player, while I'm here still grappling with where I really stand with Zane.

He keeps insisting that we can just be friends, but the tension that crackles between us whenever we're in each other's orbit is impossible to ignore.

We both feel it. The electric charge that pulses between us, teases at something more than *just friends*.

Only a girl who hasn't been burned by male friendships would trust Zane and his intentions.

But at the same time, he's been incredibly thoughtful toward both of us. It's clear he enjoys seeing Robyn happy, and I suspect it's his subtle way of trying to win me over.

He is standing in the kitchen, sleeves rolled up and the top buttons of his shirt undone. I'm doing my best to avoid looking in his general direction.

"All right, hope you all love chicken fajitas. That's what I've got going on today." He definitely whipped it up fast, since Robyn and I didn't prolong our goodbyes after the service like we usually do.

"How did he know?" Robyn squeals, shooting me a wide-eyed glance.

"Lucky guess?" Zane replies, leaning over the sink to rinse his hands.

It's definitely not luck. I've come to realize Zane picks up on a lot of things, including Robyn's and my Friday night dinners at the *Fiesta Grill*.

"Please, make yourselves at home," Zane says warmly, setting down a spread of sizzling fajita fixings on the island.

Robyn and I instinctively head to the fridge for condiments and refreshments, as if it isn't our first time here.

"Sorry about the makeshift seating. I'm in the middle of giving my dining table a coat of stain," Zane explains.

I glance behind us and notice there's ample space for a big circular table. But I didn't think someone who lives alone would need a dining table.

I settle between Zane and Robyn, with all of us facing the sink, stove, and fridge. It feels a bit awkward, like being back in church or in a classroom—none of us facing each other. We're all just focused on our plates.

Knowing Zane is right next to me, it's a bit of a struggle to enjoy these delicious tacos without making a mess.

"Did you paint these?" I finally muster the courage to ask, gesturing toward one of the frames on the wall. It's a hockey player skating away, the background a blur of motion.

I wonder if there's a deeper meaning behind this artwork beyond just Zane's love for hockey.

"Yes, I did these a while back. Haven't done anything like it since." I sense nostalgia in the way he says it.

"Why? You're clearly talented."

"I second that! You could totally sell your paintings," Robyn chimes in before adding, "Not that you'd need to."

He definitely doesn't need to. His spacious house, filled with tasteful touches of luxury, suggests that he's already quite well-off. But he should paint because he's talented and clearly has a passion for it, or at least he used to.

The conversation flows effortlessly between us, and I'm gradually finding myself comfortable around Zane.

He's really easy to talk to. Between my stories and Robyn's, I'd say he's quite the trooper for listening and asking follow-up questions.

But then again, he's a guy who doesn't believe in my Lord and Savior. I shouldn't be focusing on his qualities right now.

What was it like for him to come to church? He mentioned it wasn't his first time, but it would be his first as an adult.

As if she could read my mind, Robyn asks the question, "So, what did you think of today's service?"

I slowly turn to watch him respond, the distance between us suddenly feeling too close when our eyes meet.

I can feel the warmth of his body and his smell teases my senses, threatening to drown me if his captivating eyes or infectious smile don't do me in first.

Zane takes a sip of water, his gaze momentarily drifting to his nearly-empty plate. "I was intrigued, to say the least. I've never heard the life of Jesus explained in such a way. He was..." He pauses, searching for the right words. "He was full of love and compassion. I'm beginning to understand why people would want to follow him."

My heart skips a beat at his words. It's the first time I've heard him speak about Christianity with such openness, and now I'm curious about which part of the sermon changed his perspective.

"You understand?" My eyes lock with his, and for a moment, it feels like the world around us fades away. I forget that Robyn is part of this conversation, the one who prompted him to share all this.

"I'm starting to," he responds, his gaze holding mine with sincerity before releasing me.

Perhaps it's just wishful thinking on my part, but I can't help but feel hopeful. Maybe I'm hoping that if Zane embraces Christianity, there's a chance for us. After all, there are already so many things I admire about him.

I've been down this road before.

All Clay, my ex, had to do was express interest in knowing Jesus, and I opened my heart to him without a second thought. I didn't even take the time to really pray about it; I simply assumed it was God's will for me to date him and guide him to Christ. But in the end, he shattered my trust and broke up with me, citing my boundaries as too restrictive. I had made it clear from the start that my commitment to purity was serious, but he dismissed it, and later claimed it was something all the girls he'd been with said in the beginning of a relationship but never actually followed through. And to add insult to injury, he revealed that his interest in Jesus was nothing more than a ploy to win me over.

He never wanted to deepen his relationship with God.

What if Zane's intentions are no different?

Being here in his house shows that I've failed to follow through on my resolve after Clay. Yet, another part of me whispers that Zane may not share my faith, but he's not deceitful like Clay was. I don't know why I'm giving that stray thought more weight than it deserves.

Is this how I'm destined to fall again?

22

Zane Ortiz

"And I thought my schedule was demanding," I say to Pearl, still marveling at the fact that she's here in my kitchen, helping me load the dishwasher. I wish there'd be more moments like this, but even I know that's only happening in my dreams. Pearl has turned down all my invitations until I enlisted the help of her best friend.

I'd initially insisted she just sit and let me handle the cleaning, but after Robyn dashed off for a work phone call, Pearl seemed uncomfortable just watching me do the dishes by myself.

It's endearing how she gets flustered by even the slightest hint of awkwardness around me.

"Robs works too hard," she says, rinsing a plate. "She's gunning for a promotion to VP of finance in her company, and you can imagine the uphill battle she's facing, competing with older, more experienced men."

"I have no doubt she'll achieve her goals, especially since she's so passionate about her work. She's willing to tackle projects on a Sunday afternoon. That's impressive," I say, glancing toward the window where Robyn sits on the patio, completely focused on her laptop, which she apparently carries with her everywhere.

Pearl leans in a bit and I catch a whiff of her pleasant fruity scent. "It has nothing to do with passion." She bites her lower lip, and my eyes play out the moment she releases it in slow motion.

Focus, Zane.

She continues, "She struggles with tying her identity too closely to her job. I'm only telling you this because it's something she's open about. I would've tried to keep her from answering that phone call, but trust me, you're not ready for the heated disagreement that would follow."

I can easily imagine Pearl and Robyn getting at each other's nerves. They seem like they're the type to engage in some serious tough love, much like my teammates do. But with girls, I'm sure it's handled with a bit more sensitivity. They seem incredibly close. It's more than just a regular friendship; they really have each other's backs.

"I'm not one to judge, though," I continue, my hand finding its way to my neck as I finish putting everything in its place. "Hockey is my identity, and so far, it hasn't steered me wrong. It's what everyone knows me by, and it's the only place I feel like I belong."

"That's not true." Pearl's voice trails off as she walks toward the living room. "I don't know you as a hockey player. I know you as the stalker at Randy's café," she says laughing at her own joke.

"When we first met, I was actually just a customer." We both laugh.

It's crazy to think about all the changes that happened in just a few weeks. After a couple of encounters, I started to think I should dial back my desire to get to know Pearl. And then along came the incident with Kate and Duke, which really pushed things to where they are now. I suppose I should personally thank them—especially Duke—for not dating Pearl. The mere thought of them together makes me cringe.

"I know you're more than good in the women's department. Robyn mentioned your female fans. Why were you so persistent with me?" she asks, as if my persistence has waned.

Perhaps toning it down a bit is what's brought her here to my house. I could tell her the truth, although it's rather basic and not particularly impressive—that she's the most beautiful person I've ever laid my eyes on. It's like she has a halo above her head, and being near her feels necessary to me. She has this charm that always draws me in effortlessly. But I also don't want her to leave because I tried to flirt with her.

So, I simply reply, "What do you think it was?"

Leaning against the wall beside the couch where she's perched, our knees almost touch. She confidently says, "You're probably used to attention from women my age. So when you realized I didn't know who you were, it bruised your ego."

"Quite the therapist you are." A chortle escapes my lips. "But no, it was refreshing to find out much later that you hate hockey and didn't know me. I could use more people in my life who aren't impressed by me," I say, and she gives a cute frown. Is it normal to be so endeared by every expression on her face? "I don't mind fans. Again, I wouldn't be where I am without their support. But it just doesn't happen often in Bedford to not be put on a pedestal."

"First off, y'all have to stop with the whole *I hate hockey*. I don't. I just know it can get pretty intense sometimes, and for someone who doesn't watch any sport, violence isn't exactly my cup of tea." She winces slightly, miming an apology.

"It really doesn't bother me that it's not your thing. Maybe you don't want to say that out loud when you meet the team, but hey, it can be our little secret," I say, realizing the last part might have been a bit too forward.

"It's not a secret anymore. Robyn loves to expose me any chance she gets," she says with a mischievous glint in her eyes. "But I guess if you're on my side, I'll be safe."

A soft blush colors her cheeks, and the absence of any argument about meeting the team tells me she's done pushing me away. *At last.*

Have I finally earned a place in Pearl's good graces, or is it just the lingering effect of a good meal? She's always praised *Fiesta Grill*, and I knew anything from their menu would be a hit, but I never expected to see her this relaxed around me. And, truth be told, I'm glad that Robyn's occupied. Otherwise, I wouldn't have this chance to be alone with her.

"I have an idea. Do you want to help me stain the dining table?" I ask on a whim.

"I don't even know how to use a brush," she replies, nervously fidgeting with her fingers.

"It's super easy. I can teach you. Looks like Robyn's gonna be on that call for a while."

She agrees that it sounds like a fun way to pass the time. I ask her to give me a minute and head upstairs to change into comfortable sweats and put on a cap to protect my hair. I want to make sure Pearl doesn't stain her dress either, so I grab my newest sweats with the Glaciers logo and their matching bottoms.

After changing, I bound down the stairs. Pearl is sitting on the couch, lost in thought, her gaze fixed on the window. I wish I knew what was on her mind.

It's intriguing how she's not absorbed in her phone like everyone else I know, including myself when I'm alone. I know she isn't active on social media, but aren't there enough funny cat videos to keep anyone entertained?

When Pearl emerges from the bathroom wearing my clothes, my heart takes a cross-check. I *almost* can't breathe.

I've never been one to share my closet with anyone, but I'd definitely reconsider if Pearl wants to borrow all my clothes.

"I'm not sure I'll give it back. It's super cozy," she says, her hands lost in the sleeves.

"Keep it. It looks better on you," I reply, trying my best to hide the grin on my face.

Pearl snorts. She isn't petite at all, but her feminine curves are completely hidden in my clothes. She looks absolutely adorable.

I lead her to the garage where the dining table is, and with a swift motion, I sweep away the tarp covering the table. I arrange the supplies closer to her—an assortment of brushes, the dark walnut stain, and a container of water for cleaning the brushes.

Pearl takes the brush and holds it by the handle's top, and I smile, realizing it's probably her first time doing a DIY project like this.

"Here, let me show you how to hold the brush," I say, gently guiding her hands closer to the bristles. The touch of her fingers against mine sends my heart racing.

I demonstrate a few brushstrokes on the tabletop, and she looks at me with beaming eyes, her gaze intent as she watches me work. I gesture for her to give it a go.

She hesitates at first but then begins with a small stroke. As she gains confidence, her eagerness shows, but in her excitement, she accidentally smudges a spot. Her expression shifts to concern.

"Oh no, this doesn't look right," she says, flinching.

"Don't worry, nothing you can't fix." I show her how to smooth out the smudged area and she does a pretty decent job at it.

Her focused expression, the way her blonde curls gently fall over her face, and the subtle bite of her lips make me wonder what it would be like to turn her angelic face and kiss her. I quickly shake my head.

Friends.

We agreed on friendship. *For now.*

Lost in this amazing world where Pearl is doing a project with me in my garage, we enjoy a comfortable silence. My gaze isn't as focused on the dining table as it should be because Pearl is proving herself capable of the task. She's not even sparing me a glance, which is giving me ample opportunity to study her every feature.

One of her eyebrows has a slight raise to it, giving her this endearing quirk. And until today, I hadn't noticed the barely-there freckles that are only visible up close. Her eyes are that perfect almond shape, with a cute, petite nose that's got a little point to it. I'm doing my best to steer clear of her full lips, but it's proving to be a challenge. If it wasn't for Robyn's warning earlier, I'd have caved a long time ago. But I desperately need her to trust me. I need to make it easier for her to get there.

She shifts slightly, getting down on her knees to reach the back side of the table, a delicate crease forming between her brows as she concentrates. Every time a drip of stain slides off the brush and hits the floor, she quickly dabs it with a rag. It's beyond sweet how perfectly she wants to do this. While it may be taking longer to stain this table than it would have if I hadn't been putting it off for a while, Pearl's presence and the little quirks of her efforts make this feel less like a task and more like a moment I want to capture and hold onto forever.

Suddenly, Robyn's voice interrupts us, pulling me back to reality.

"I wanted to say I'm ready to go, but y'all look like you just started your project," she says, hinting at something else.

Pearl's demeanor completely changes, as if she's trying to snap herself out of this dream too.

"No, I think I've done enough damage to this table. Let's go home," she says, replacing her enthusiasm with an all too familiar distant tone.

Was the fun we were having all in my head? Why is Pearl trying to resist enjoying herself with me?

23

♥

Pearl Davis

On any given day, I'd rather not go through the trouble of packing my own lunch, but if there's even the slightest chance I might run into Zane, well, Randy's isn't an option anymore.

Enduring another sip of my mediocre coffee is only adding to the headache already pulsing in my temples. But then again, that's a small price to pay to avoid falling for Zane.

Yesterday, when he taught me how to stain a table, was one of the sweetest moments I've ever shared with anyone, and it wasn't even a date. In fact, I have no business doing anything romantic with that guy.

According to the unspoken rules of whatever this is between us, we're not even supposed to be hanging out. How am I supposed to maintain any semblance of composure around someone who turns my knees to jelly with just a smile?

Whenever Zane looks at me, it's as if time slows to a crawl, and I'm left gasping for air like a fish out of water. He is kind, he smells amazing, he can cook—basically, he's a walking list of all the things women want in a man.

All this swooning shouldn't blind me from the glaring truth that we're unequally yoked, and I need to distance myself from him, pronto. It's a deal breaker for me, and the last thing I want is for him to turn into another Clay.

Maybe he's the type to recite the sinner's prayer just to win me over for a fling.

And while the thought of only a fling with him breaks my heart, I've done enough digging to know his track record with relationships. They rarely last more than a few months, if that, and who's to say he's not already entangled in one on the down-low? No, thank you. I refuse to get caught up in that kind of mess.

The fact that I finally managed to get him a referral to a sports counselor I went to school with is a sign that I've fulfilled my purpose in his life. This must be the only reason why God allowed our paths to cross.

My phone chimes with a new message. It's Zane.

Zane

> Dinner at my house tomorrow? Let Robyn know. I'll have a few friends over. Tell her it's Tyler and Carson. She'll be thrilled.

Pearl

> Robyn doesn't get home 'til after dinner. She has a busy week.

THE GAME SHE HATES

Zane

> You're still welcome to come.

Pearl

> Not a good idea. What am I going to talk about with a bunch of hockey players?

Zane

> You and I communicate okay, don't we? Actually, you'll find more common ground with them than you do with me.

Pearl

> Are you saying I'll like your friends more than I like you?

Zane

> Sweet P. Are you telling me you like me? If so, I think a confession like that deserves more than just a text message.

I deserve a punch in the face for that. Why am I flirting with Zane? This isn't the pep talk I've been giving myself.

It has to end now.

> **Pearl**
> Listen. I found a sports counselor for you. Dr. Lawson is great. I personally know him from my college days. You will like him. P.S. He is a believer; not sure how much of his faith is woven into his practice, but I thought you needed to know.

> **Zane**
> Is this a yes, you like me and you found me a counselor? Or no, you don't, so you found me a counselor so I never have to talk to you again?

Why is Zane pushing all the buttons today? Goodness.

> **Pearl**
> I still don't think we can be friends, Zane.

> **Zane**
> You've said it from the beginning, but despite that, we've been getting along pretty great. Except for how abruptly you left yesterday. I thought we were having a good time together. I, for one, was.

That's exactly the issue. I'm failing to stick to my decision, and before I know it, I'll be in too deep.

Pearl

> I gotta get ready for my client. Sorry about bailing tonight. Please see Dr. Lawson. Bye.

I silence my phone and place it in a drawer, resisting the temptation to check for Zane's reply. With closed eyes and hands pressed to my face, I pray. "God, I know that Zane has found a place in my heart, but I don't want to endure more pain. I trust that the man You have destined for me is someone who has walked faithfully with You for as long as I have, if not longer, and lives in alignment with Your will. I need a husband who is a spiritual leader and who understands the profound sacrifice You made on Calvary. Please guide me to this person."

·♥·♥·♥·♥·♥·

I finish up my nighttime routine in the bathroom, the sweet scent of vanilla and honey lingers in my freshly washed hair. I reach for a towel and lightly pat my skin dry, still feeling the faint dampness from the shower. I wrap the towel around my head and secure it in place to soak up the remaining moisture.

Suddenly, a noise echoes from the living room, stopping the hum I had going on. My heart skips a beat; it's too early for Robyn to be back.

With a quick prayer, I step out of the bathroom.

Why is Robyn home early and leaning against the door like she lost someone?

"Hey, are you okay?" I ask, concerned. "I thought this week was supposed to be all work and no sleep?"

Robyn pushes herself off the door, her heavy handbag landing with a thud on the couch. "This guy took over my project. It's going to be a slower week," she replies, her pixie-like features contorted in frustration.

I join her on the couch, offering what comfort I can. "I'm sorry. How did he manage to take your project?"

"The CEO appointed him project manager, and initially, we were working on it together. But after last night, he basically didn't sleep and pushed the project forward without me."

"I know you hate when people do that. But, hey, at least you won't have to run on two hours of sleep and espresso," I say, trying to find the silver lining.

"That's the only way I'll ever become VP. Not all of us have marriage and family aspirations like you." Her gaze drifts away.

I tenderly take both of her hands in mine. Her work always seems to hit her hard. I wish I could help her see that there's more to life than just her career.

"You know, marriage and kids are a gift from the Lord, and He wants it for most of us," I say softly.

"You said it, most, not all," she counters. "I'm going to be like Paul. Marrying makes people lose focus on the things that are more important, and it gives power to another human over your life. Not exactly what I want out of this life."

I pause for a moment, allowing the Holy Spirit to guide my words. Some days, Robyn and I banter and debate over our differing perspectives on life, but on others, we sharpen each other like iron. And today, I believe that what she needs is the truth.

"You're purposefully taking 1 Corinthians chapter 7 completely out of context to justify your biggest fear," I gently explain. "Paul says being single is good for him because he was fully invested in doing God's work around the clock. But we both know that's not why you don't want marriage."

She rolls her eyes. She knows I'm right, even if she hates confronting the reason behind her aversion to marriage.

"Speaking of marriage, did you talk to Zane?" Hearing Robyn mention marriage and Zane in the same breath makes my heart skip. But I did tell her last night about my decision to distance myself from him before I fall for him completely. Maybe she thinks I want to marry him. After all, I'm known for loving commitment.

It just doesn't love me the same.

"He texted, inviting us to his house tomorrow. Used you as bait, obviously." Now it was my turn to roll my eyes.

"It really sucks that Zane Ortiz has to be in love with my best friend, and now I get to be involved in ditching him. My life is *so* hard." She jerks her head backward in fake frustration. The change of subject seems to have lifted her spirits.

"He isn't in love with me. He can't be. We barely have anything in common," I murmur, trying to convince myself as much. "And I guess this isn't a good time to mention he wanted us to hang out with his friends Tyler and Carson," I add hesitantly.

Robyn shoots up from the couch. "Stop it right now, Pearl Davis. My favorite trio? Are you sure you don't want to break up with him, like, on Wednesday? I want to meet them so bad." She puts a finger on her chin, as if she's in deep thought. "Wait, not next week because you don't want to do that before their game on Thursday. It'd be bad luck, and you cannot ruin their winning streak. Zane Ortiz needs to be on his A-game."

"You really took this whole thing out of proportion, didn't you. Break up? When did we become boyfriend and girlfriend in the first place?" I raise both my arms in exasperation.

"I don't know what else to call it. The guy is clearly into you. He's not like some of the other guys on his team, always chasing after women. And you, I'm not blind. I know you are avoiding him because you don't want to let on that you're into him too."

"He's just a man used to girls falling at his feet, and he finally found someone who doesn't find his game and everything he stands for that impressive."

Robyn settles back into her seat, locking eyes with me. "Come to the game with me on Thursday. If you still think he's unimpressive after that, I'll never tell anyone you hate hockey. I'll just keep it to myself that my bestie is deranged."

I laugh. "You're joking, right? I'm already not talking to him, and now you want me to go cheer him on? Do you realize what kind of mixed signals that sends? He'll definitely think I'm into him."

"But you totally are," she winces. "But seriously, we won't sit in VIP; he can't see everyone in the stands. We'll leave right after the game."

"Why should I agree to this?" I'm so confused that we're even having this conversation. Robyn has never invited me to a game before. She knows I won't even watch it on TV. Although I did once at Kate's, but she doesn't know that. Maybe she's asking because she's certain a part of me wants to go see Zane in his element. She wouldn't be wrong.

"You're not as apprehensive as I thought you'd be," she quickly adds. "So it's a done deal. I'll even get you a ticket. You don't have to worry about a single thing." She flashes one of her signature big grins, knowing she's gotten her way.

How did I agree to this?

24

Zane Ortiz

It's just me and Tyler left in the gym. With everyone else having gone home after our lifting session, I seize the chance to ask him to stick around and join me on the stationary bike.

I've been wanting to pick his brain about my recent thoughts, but I haven't found the perfect moment to broach the subject. Every time I've tried to bring it up, someone has interrupted us during our workout.

"What did you want to ask earlier?" Tyler asks, pedaling slowly. The goal isn't to raise our heart rates, that's for sure.

A feeling of timidity floods over me for a few seconds, but I remind myself that Tyler is the best person to ask about this. He's been a friend when I wanted to know nothing about his faith, and he'll walk me through my roadblocks without judgment.

"I don't understand why God became a man to come to this world to die for our sins. Couldn't he have maybe come to eradicate all the suffering instead?" I finally say, feeling a bit vulnerable.

A curve forms on Tyler's mouth, his smile lines betraying the few years he has on us. "I know suffering seems like the world's worst problem to us. But not to God. Sin is his biggest concern. It's what brought suffering into the world back in Eden, and it's what continues to perpetuate it. Sin is the one thing that separates God from human beings because He can't coexist with it. That's why He sent Adam and Eve out of Eden. After creating them and seeing that it was good, it must have broken His heart not to have a relationship with them. The only way to bridge that gap was through the sacrifice Jesus made on Calvary."

I blink twice, trying to absorb this new information.
Dying for a relationship with us?
"What does a relationship with God actually mean?"
Tyler leans back slightly. "It means that after believing that Jesus is your Lord and Savior—acknowledging that He died for your sins—you can have fellowship with God," he explains thoughtfully.

I widen my eyes. "In layman's terms, please."

"When you have a relationship with God, He is with you all the time." He clears his throat. "When you're suffering, He's there to comfort and ease your pain, granting you peace amid life's storms. When doubt creeps in, He strengthens your faith. When you're lost, He guides you. You never have to face anything alone when you have a relationship with God."

I feel a lump form in my throat as I'm about to share a piece of my pain with him. "Sometimes, I feel like no one can comfort the suffering I've endured. Never knowing my mom, and feeling responsible for her death in some way... It's a burden no one I've ever met can understand. No one knows what it's like to walk that path. It's made me question if this life is worth..." I trail off, noticing his expression softening. "It didn't help that I grew up with a dad who liked to remind me of the pain I brought into this world when I was born."

Tyler extends his hand to rest on my shoulder. "I'm sorry. I can't even begin to imagine how hard it's been for you all these years. And I understand wanting someone else to fully understand your pain, but that doesn't guarantee healing. Only Jesus heals." He continues. "The Bible calls Him a man acquainted with sorrow. He faced suffering of all kinds, and I know for sure grief was one of them, having lost His earthly father and later a close friend whom He resurrected."

He then dismounts from the bike, reaches into his pocket for his phone, and continues. "There's a Bible verse my family and I always turn to in hard and painful seasons that reminds us to go to Jesus. It's from Hebrews 4:15-16: *'For we do not have a high priest who cannot sympathize with our weaknesses, but One who has been tempted in all things just as we are, yet without sin. Therefore let's approach the throne of grace with confidence, so that we may receive mercy and find grace for help at the time of our need.'*"

I'm amazed at how Tyler and Pearl have these Bible verses memorized. The Bible seems like a dense book and full of history, but when I hear these quotes, they're exactly what I need at that precise moment.

"Thanks for sharing that," I say. "Do you really think anyone can have a relationship with God? I mean, I've been unkind to people who didn't deserve it—all in the name of trying to get even with the hand I've been dealt. I've pushed away people in my life who tried to care. Do you think I deserve this Christian life too?"

Tyler shakes his head, "You don't deserve it, but neither do I. Nobody deserves the love God showed us on Calvary. He had His son suffer in our place. What we all deserved was to be on that cross. And I'm grateful God doesn't give us what we deserve; that's why salvation is a gift. We can't earn His love, so neither of us can boast about doing something right."

"How do I start this relationship with God?" I ask.

"You ask Him to come into your heart as soon as you believe in what He did. When you truly believe and invite Him in, He will come into your life. Then, you'll need to exercise faith to believe it—it's a continuous process of trusting and relying on Him. Building a relationship with God happens when you engage with His Word; it's the primary way to know His nature and His will for us.

"When you receive the Holy Spirit, the Bible becomes alive and relevant, revealing more about Jesus Christ, whom we strive to emulate. As you grow closer to Him, you'll naturally desire to avoid actions that would hurt Him—not out of fear of punishment, but out of genuine love and reverence. When you get a glimpse of God's love for you, you'll not want to spend this life or eternity without your Creator and lover of your soul."

Whoa, my mind just expanded with this conversation.

If starting a relationship with Jesus is this straightforward, I should've taken notes when Tyler was talking. He really said some interesting things. I hope I don't forget any of it.

"I have to ask, bro. What's with all these questions all of a sudden?" I've also stopped pedaling.

"I went to church once, and I've been replaying the sermon the pastor preached in my mind since that day," I reply, leaving out some important details.

"Why didn't you tell me you've been going to church? And what changed your mind? I've been inviting you for ages, and just when I'd given up, you finally give it a try. I mean, I'm happy but also super convicted that I stopped asking."

"No, I'm glad you stopped asking. I don't think I was ever going to change my mind," I pause, deciding to let it all spill out. "I met this girl. She invited me to church, and I honestly went just to see her since she didn't want to hang out with me. Well, I guess you'd say God used my interest in a girl to show me He's interested in me too."

"Who is this girl, and more importantly, why haven't we met her yet?" he says, hands up in the air as if I said I was dating her or something. He's going to be disappointed.

"Never mind who she is. She wants zero to do with me," I reply, making a zero sign with my hands to emphasize her complete disinterest. "For a while, I thought we were becoming friends and had some hope, but she's completely ghosted me. I guess I'm really not her type." It had been a few days since Pearl sent me a message about the counselor she'd found for me, which was great. I'd met him briefly on a video call, but I missed Pearl so much. I tried to call, text, but she wasn't replying, and the message was clear.

I thought having her at my house and just hanging out with her, not pulling out overtly flirty moves, at least as best as I could, would help her trust that I wasn't just physically attracted to her. But I guess there wasn't any way for her to trust someone like me.

I was a fool for getting my hopes up when I discovered she wasn't a fan of hockey, thinking maybe she'd appreciate me for who I am. Yet, now it's clear there's nothing about me to admire, except my skills on the ice and the way I handle the puck. Apart from that, I'm just an empty canvas.

It's time to cut my losses and give her the space she *strongly* desires.

I need to focus on finding my own path to fulfillment, much like Tyler, Carson, and even Coach seem to have found in their relationship with God through Jesus.

Tonight, I'll say the prayer. I'll ask Jesus to come into my life. I need to finally know what it's like to have a good Father.

· ♥ · ♥ · ♥ · ♥ · ♥ ·

The semi-final game is a fierce battle, with our opponent proving to be a tough challenge. Sticks clash, the crowd roars, and the pressure mounts with every passing second. I'm being closed in from all sides, struggling to break free for even a moment.

I scan the stands for encouragement, hoping to find fans in my jersey. Maybe seeing them will remind me that I can score two more goals to win this game. But then, amidst the sea of faces, one catches my eye.

No, it can't be her.

Pearl would never be at a hockey game.

She hates hockey.

She hates sports.

She hates me.

Well, maybe *hate* is a strong word for a Christian. She definitely doesn't like me.

That can't be her at my game, in *my* jersey.

But there can't be another face as beautiful as hers on this planet. That's the face that always takes my breath away. It's the one I hate to have gone so many days without seeing.

A quick glance to her right confirms that it is indeed her with Robyn and the jersey she's wearing is the one I gave Robyn.

Out of nowhere, a surge of energy courses through me, invigorating my limbs and sharpening my focus. The weight of the game falls away and is replaced by a newfound desire to win, fueled by the sight of Pearl.

If this is what it feels like to play with someone you're a fan of, cheering for you, I'll give Robyn whatever she wants to make sure Pearl comes to the final game.

I charge forward, dodging opponents with emerging agility. Hunter receives the puck, passing quickly to Fabrice, who redirects it to Trent. Tyler and I skate ahead, seizing the momentum.

When the play shifts in our favor, I see my opportunity.

I take the shot, the puck sails through the air toward the goal, and in that moment, everything slows down. The crowd holds its breath as the puck hits the net.

Goal!

25
♥

Pearl Davis

The crowd erupts after Zane's goal, but I stand frozen—not because of the deafening cheers, but because Zane's eyes are locked onto me. He wears this grateful and somehow flirty expression, as if those goals he just scored have something to do with me.

I can't believe he spotted me in this crowd. How did he even know where to look? The first time his eyes found me, I thought I was gonna pass out.

I had a feeling that coming to this game was a bad idea. It wasn't fair or smart to subject my poor heart to watching Zane play when I was trying so hard to move on from him.

Robyn had convinced me there was no way he could spot us from where we were sitting. Well, she was wrong—very wrong. Now, I definitely regret coming here.

I wonder what he's thinking. I've been ghosting him for days, and now here I am at his game, wearing his jersey, all because my persuasive best friend insisted it was a fan tradition. Robyn had an extra one she got from Zane, so she convinced me I'd fit right in if I wore it.

The way he's looking at me... It's making it hard to hide this smile and the heat rushing to my face. How am I going to convince him that I want nothing to do with him after this.

"What was that?" Robyn exclaims, her voice raspy and strained from hours of screaming and cheering.

Both teams have already left the ice. They departed after a joyous celebration from the Glaciers that included gloves and sticks tossed in the air.

"What?" I ask, feigning ignorance. The glances Zane threw in my direction were hard to miss.

"You know what I'm talking about! Did you and Zane just have a moment? I mean, moments? Every time he scored, he basically dedicated the goal to you." A smirk is playing at the corners of her lips as she calls me out.

"I saw him looking this way. Look at all these women wearing his number," I deflect, my gaze shifting to the fans filtering out of the arena. Some head toward the locker rooms, eager to catch a glimpse of their favorite players and maybe even get an autograph or two.

Robyn's knowing expression doesn't escape me; she sees right through my feeble attempt to deny the obvious.

"I've been at every one of his games. That's not Zane Ortiz. When he looks into the stands, he never zeroes in on one person. And the way he played the whole game... I promise, it's like he was a different guy out there."

"What do you mean?" I ask, puzzled by her assertion. Zane only seemed to notice me toward the end of the game, so I'm certain I'm not the one behind this new player.

"He played differently, his usual anger and edge were lacking, but there was also this new intensity about him. I can't quite explain it. But what I can say with conviction is that he is absolutely smitten with my roommate." Robyn's words finally punctuate our conversation as she stands up.

We wait a moment to exit, letting the crowd thin out a little. Most are in a hurry to beat the traffic, but our drive from Boston to Bedford isn't bad at all.

As we make our way out of the arena and into the cool night air, we slide into the car. Robyn takes the driver's seat. I'm glad she's driving. Navigating through this crowd of loud hockey fanatics seems too risky for me.

"P, tell me the truth. Do you have feelings for Zane Ortiz?" Robyn asks, her eyes focused on the road as traffic eases up. If she were watching my reaction right now, she'd know the answer to this question. Robyn can read me very well.

"I can't have feelings for Zane. You know that."

"But you do," she says, her tone more of a statement than a question.

There's no point in denying it. I haven't stopped thinking about him no matter how much I've tried to distance myself.

Admitting to liking him feels like betraying myself, my past experiences, and what I've learned from dating guys like him.

But God sees my heart. Robyn has an inkling too. I'm not fooling anyone.

"I like him, and I don't know how to stop."

"I didn't need you to confirm you liked him. I *knew* it. It was selfish of me to take you to the game. I'm sorry. I just wanted us to keep him." She purses her lips.

"Keep him? He's not a stray puppy, Robs," I laugh, feeling some relief.

"I mean keep him in our circle, you know? I think he's a pretty great guy, and not just because I've always been Team Zane Ortiz. Zane off the ice is pretty cool too."

I sense the sincerity in her voice.

"I wish my feelings didn't have to complicate things. I know you weren't thrilled with our seats. You were probably getting used to great views with Zane's tickets."

The last two games, Robyn managed to score VIP tickets from Zane. I'm really ruining things for her.

"What do you mean? Watching a game with you was on my bucket list."

"Come on, Robs. It can't be that important to you."

"We've practically done everything together except this. Just think about it." She's right. We've done so many things together, except watch hockey.

"But listen." She clears her throat, "I understand your reservations about Zane. You're worried he'll turn out like Clay. But he's different. Despite all the silence, he's been patient with you. He's still here and he watched you from a distance like he was scoring just for you. And despite all the attention he gets from other women, he hasn't given in to any of them. I'm just saying that you've always been all about real love and romance, and it seems like Zane might be embodying that."

Robyn is usually the one stopping me from getting into relationships. Her admiration for Zane as her favorite player might be the one speaking.

"You told me he keeps a really low profile, so who knows if he really isn't giving in to these fans of his. Anyway, whether his feelings are real or not, we can't work, and you know that. He doesn't believe in God. Our whole worldview is different. *'Do not be unequally yoked with unbelievers. For what partnership has righteousness with lawlessness? Or what fellowship has light with darkness.'* 2 Corinthians 6:14. God breathed this word for me and for my situation. I can't turn a blind eye just because Zane is basically eye candy and has all these great qualities."

"The fact that he came to church makes me think he's not that apprehensive about knowing God. Maybe give him that opportunity. Invite him to church again. You never know how and when the Lord will reveal Himself to people."

"No, it's too risky. I've had my fill of turning my dating life into a conversion project. I need to *guard my heart above all else.* I know my soulmate is out there, praying, asking God to bring his future wife and hoping I'm ignoring the wrong men that come looking like Zane. I can't keep investing in relationships where faith misaligns."

Even after saying this, the thought of another guy entering my life doesn't quite sit right.

Goodness!

How do I have it this bad for a hockey player, of all professions. And not just any, but a wildly popular one.

It's ironic, really. Here I am—someone who prefers to blend into the background, remain unnoticed and unseen, always occupying the last row in school and church to evade unnecessary attention—now pining for everyone's celebrity crush.

My heart couldn't have orchestrated a better prank if it tried.

· ♥ · ♥ · ♥ · ♥ · ♥ ·

During dinner, Robyn gave up trying to convince me to talk to Zane. I know she understands me, her relationship with Jesus also comes first and she'd do the same if she was in my shoes. Not that I can imagine her catching feelings for a man. All the years I've known her, she only knows how to scare them away. I wish I could be more like her, and keep my heart under wraps instead of wearing it on my sleeve.

After my shower, I head to my room. Robyn's working on her project, finally having found her groove again with her team. I feel for her, I could never be in an industry as harsh. At least she knows how to stand up for herself.

I, on the other hand, have the best career in the world, rivaled only by pediatricians.

Working with children who are navigating different challenges as they try to find their forever homes has always been my dream. When I sense even a glimmer of affection from a child's family, I make it my duty to help the child see it too. As someone who once lost hope before finding

Beatrice and Fynn, I refuse to let these children miss out on the chance of an amazing family or have to bear the weight of their heavy baggage alone. It's not their fault. They didn't choose the life they've been dealt.

I pick up my devotional, hoping it will lull me into sleep, when my phone vibrates in my drawer, causing my heart to skip a beat.

It's around the time when Zane would typically call, but it's been a few days of silence. Part of me is relieved he's stopped calling since I wasn't picking up, but another part of me has ached at the absence of his name on my screen every night.

My feelings are frustratingly complex.

I stretch my arm and open the drawer, surprised that I even forgot to silence my phone before I went to bed, something I always do. Maybe, a part of me did hope Zane would reach out.

The message from Zane pops up on my screen:

Zane

> Thanks for coming to the game. You have no idea how much I needed that.

My heart swells at his message, and I'm tempted to pour out my feelings to him. I wouldn't mind watching him play for the rest of his career. Seeing him on ice was one of the most exhilarating experiences of my life. My eyes were glued on him, following his every move with ease, more effortlessly than when I watched him play on TV. He was amazing and a hundred times hotter than I already knew him to be.

But I bottle it all up inside. Each conversation with him threatens to unravel my true feelings, and I can't contradict all the days I've dedicated to avoiding him. It would seem as though all my suffering was for nothing—and probably his too.

Jesus, help me discern what to do with my heart. I've tried everything I know, but I'm at a standstill. All I want is to honor You in my relationships and bring glory to Your name. I know Zane can't be my person because he doesn't know You. Help him find You, Lord. I know I'm asking for selfish reasons, but I know You care about him even more than I do. You care about everyone's soul. Please save his. Amen.

I put my phone on silent, place it back in the drawer, close my eyes, and images of Zane flood my mind as I drift off to sleep.

26

Pearl Davis

The atmosphere at Kate's bridal shower is nothing short of magical. All of us bridesmaids came together to create a simple, yet elegant setting, perfectly matching the wedding colors of gold and teal. We transformed Carole's house into one beautiful venue, adorned with lilies and roses on the round tables, along with scripture cards and games.

Carole, one of the elder's wives, had eagerly offered to host the shower.

Worship music plays softly in the background, and the scent of Carole's delicious food fills the air, reminding me that lunch was ages ago. With laughter and chatter filling the room, Carole initiates the scripture trivia on marriage.

I try my best not to be overzealous, and hold back from answering with the correct scripture references each time. Kate has to take the trophy. After all, she's the bride, and this day is all about celebrating her.

I pretend to be as stumped as Robyn is. She really couldn't tell you where any verse is located except for the Proverbs 31 woman.

Kate is beaming, radiating pure happiness, and I can't help but feel a surge of joy knowing that we could make this day special for her. Despite not having much family, she's poured her heart into serving the church, leading worship, and being involved in as many groups as possible. The presence of everyone here is a testament to how much we've got her back, just as she's always had ours.

As each person takes turns sharing their thoughts about Kate, I'm stung by a feeling of regret, remembering the time I was jealous of her and her relationship with Duke. In hindsight, I realize that they're truly a perfect match. Both are outgoing, they thrive in the spotlight, and exude confidence in their own skin.

It's not that I'm filled with insecurity, but as someone who's not known for having a tiny waist, I've spent far too long wishing I looked like Kate, Robyn, or any of these thin bridesmaids. It's why I've always gravitated toward loose clothing, and the thought of wearing the tight teal dress for the wedding in a couple of weeks makes me anxious. The moment I tried it on, instead of feeling beautiful, I felt self-conscious.

Oh, how I wish I could imprint the words of Psalm 139:14—'*I praise you because I am fearfully and wonderfully made*'—in my heart and mind forever.

When it's finally my turn to speak about Kate, I speak from my heart. "Kate, I see what Duke sees in you. And I know we all do. You're a servant. You speak your mind."

I pause, a fleeting thought about her lack of sensitivity crossing my thoughts, but I quickly push it aside—no one person is perfect. "You love people, and above all, you love and live for Jesus. I think you'll make an amazing wife," I conclude, a genuine smile spreading across my face.

A pink flush creeps onto Kate's cheeks. She definitely wasn't expecting such heartfelt words from me. She has probably realized that we've drifted apart over the past few months. We weren't very close but we hung out even less when her and Duke became a couple. I'm the one who created the distance, I thought it was safe as I worked on letting Duke go from my heart.

And now, there's another guy, one who's currently occupying a larger space in my heart than Duke ever did, and he refuses to budge. Maybe it was easier to move on from Duke because he was already in a serious relationship. Maybe I need to convince myself that Zane is dating someone else too. But, Duke never wanted to have anything to do with me. In fact, he may not have even realized that I liked him.

Zane wants me in a way that terrifies me, because my heart longs for him just as deeply, if not more.

After a nice message from Carole about the gift of marriage and the importance of keeping Christ at the center, she takes her seat, and Gracie, another older woman from church, rises to share her thoughts before we conclude with a prayer.

"I see that all of Kate's close friends are still single, and I want to share something important with them too. Never underestimate the season of singleness. It's not a hindrance. It's a gift from the Lord, just like marriage is."

I glance at Robyn, who now wears a grin on her face as she listens intently. But I have a feeling she'll be disappointed with whatever Gracie has to say because I've heard her speak in women's groups, and she's the biggest marriage advocate.

"Don't spend your single days wishing them away, longing for the next thing. Marriage is indeed a beautiful union, but it also demands daily sacrifice and selflessness; your spouse will come first. And when you're blessed with children, it'll be time to pour daily and intensively into them.

"So, with all my heart, I encourage you to embrace your singleness, go on adventures with Jesus and your friends, grow in your faith, and prepare your heart to welcome the right person. Trust in God's timing, for when the right person comes along, it will be in His perfect way.

"You need not feel rushed or pressured, even though us older folks at church might pry a bit. We're just curious because we love to relive our younger days through you, but never think for a minute that if you're still single and haven't found your match, there is something wrong with you. God's timing is divine, unlike our own. He's proved it time and time again in His word." She pauses, letting her words sink in. "But I must also add a word to those who fear marriage. When it's God-ordained and centered on Jesus, it will be your heaven on this earth. Okay, that was my spiel, as the young people say."

We all nod as she takes back her seat, and I blink a tear.

Every time she mentioned the right person, Zane came to my mind. But would it be heaven on earth if Jesus isn't our shared center?

27
♥

Zane Ortiz

When Duke first extended an invitation to his wedding a few weeks back, I didn't think I was gonna go. He texted me after the semi-final, congratulating me like we became best friends, but I still couldn't shake the memory of how he belittled Pearl at his engagement party. I wanted nothing to do with him.

But as days turned into weeks, and I found myself completely cut off from Pearl's life, I started to reconsider. Maybe attending Duke's wedding would give me a chance to catch a glimpse of her, perhaps even briefly talk to her.

So, a few days ago, I reached out to him and asked if the invitation still stood. He answered in record time, saying it'd be his honor to have me there.

That semi-final was supposed to be one of the best games of my life, until I stepped out of the locker room and lost sight of Pearl. My mind still wonders why she even showed up. She didn't say hi and never responded to my text thanking her.

Seeing her there gave me the willpower to push through that last period because I thought she came to watch me. I mean, she was wearing my number for crying out loud.

I don't know what I'm missing with her. The way she looks at me contradicts the distance she gives me.

I didn't bother trying to call because she had resolved not to answer my calls, even before the game.

I stand in front of my closet, deliberating between a charcoal gray and navy suit for the wedding. My phone suddenly rings on the bed. Glancing over, I see Aunt Melissa's name flashing on the screen. It's been a month, and I've been meaning to call her, but time always slipped away. There's so much I need to catch her up on.

"Hi, Aunt Mel!" I greet enthusiastically.

"Hi, sweetheart. I hope this is a good time to call," Aunt Melissa's voice comes through the phone. A sinking feeling settles in my stomach. This isn't her usual way of starting conversations. She always asks how I'm doing first.

"It is. You sound like something is wrong."

She sighs heavily. "I wouldn't be calling you about this if I didn't think it was a good idea. Your dad's been released and he really wants to talk to you."

I let out an exasperated huff. I've severed all ties with that man ages ago. If kids could divorce parents, I would've expunged his DNA from my system long ago. I have no desire to see someone who has only brought harm since the day I was born.

"Aunt Mel, I don't consider myself related to that man anymore," I say, trying to keep my tone steady.

"I know he hurt you. He knows it too, that's why he hasn't reached out."

"Not reaching out to me since I gained my independence from him has been his MO."

"No, Zane, this time he knows it, and he wants to apologize. He's changed."

My eyes practically roll out of their sockets. "Apologize? How does someone apologize for tormenting their child? Please, tell me if you know."

All this talk dampens my mood. For the past couple of weeks, nothing had been able to weigh down my heart. I felt invincible. Finally free. Not even Trent's attitude, or the relentless hustle of life, or missing Pearl had managed to drag me back into the depths of the ocean I'd been pulled from since I accepted Jesus into my life.

"Jesus saved him, Zane. I've known your dad for most of my life, and the Ortiz I've been meeting with this week is someone new, someone transformed. Someone who acknowledges all the hurt they've caused. He wants nothing more than to be heard."

All this time, I'd been thinking Aunt Melissa was on my side. Being my mom's older sister, she should be looking out for me like she always had. But now, after one encounter with my "saved" dad, she chooses his feelings over mine.

I know God is forgiving, and He's forgiven me, but I haven't done anything close to what my dad has done. I don't think a guy like him can stop himself from hurting people.

I've always aspired to be a better man, so following Jesus is the only path for me to become the man I've always wanted to be. A man entirely different from my dad. But Dad—not once in his life did he ever strive to do a single good thing. How could he even consider Jesus? Jesus, who preached the gospel of love, kindness and self-control?

"I'm not interested. Listen, I have a wedding to attend and I'm running late. Talk to you later," I say hastily, not allowing her the chance to insist, and then hang up.

I toss the phone onto my bed and sink to the edge, my hands running down my face in frustration. I didn't even get the chance to share my testimony with her.

Dad ruined that, just like he ruins everything.

But this new chapter of my life has to be different.

The sermon I watched on Sunday—I didn't attend in person to avoid making Pearl uncomfortable, since the last thing I want is for her to think I'm on my faith journey to get close to her—talked about the old passing away and the new being here. That's what it'll be from now on.

No more letting Dad control me from afar. No more allowing him to dictate my mood, stoke my anger, and embitter me about life. This is my second chance, the clean slate I've been given, and I don't want anything that would drag me back into the depths of despair.

I clasp my hands together and bring them to my forehead, the same way I saw Tyler do it the two times I've joined his Bible study. "Hi, God, it's me again. Hopefully, You're getting used to my attempts to piece together a prayer. I know I'm not as articulate as Tyler or Carson, or any of their friends. But I have a feeling You care more about the sincerity of my heart than the eloquence of my words. So I trust my jumbled prayers have been reaching You fine. I need Your help with this situation with my dad. I love Aunt Mel, and I have no doubt she cares about me, but please help her see that my dad only has bad intentions. Help her not to be deceived by him. I've lived with him longer and I know he's capable of breaking her heart now that she believes he's changed. Protect her heart when that happens, and help me remain calm the next time we talk. She'll be happy to know I've found faith in Jesus. I pray the conversation is special and not tainted by my dad. Thank You for listening to me for the third time today. I'll be back with another praise or request. Amen."

With a clearer mind, I finally decide on the navy suit, as if I needed to consult with God before making up my mind. After applying some aftershave and running a comb through my hair, I grab my black shoes and slide them on.

I'm certain the ceremony will be halfway through when I get there, so I quickly head out.

· ♥ · ♥ · ♥ · ♥ · ♥ ·

I snagged a last row seat in the ceremony, but even from far away, my vision is fixed on one of the bridesmaids who completely steals the air from my lungs. Pearl might as well be the one in white because Duke and Kate only received a single glance from me.

Pearl looks beyond stunning in her teal dress. She's typically pleasantly feminine in her clothing, but I've never seen her in a dress that hugs her curves like this one does—her amazing form on display for all to see.

I am scanning the groomsmen, wondering if any of them are as entranced by Pearl's beauty as I am. It's hard to tell which girl they're looking at, but with Pearl looking like that, she'll probably have a hard time keeping guys at bay tonight. Unless a knight in shining armor swoops in to help her navigate the evening.

Everyone erupts in applause when the groom kisses the bride. They exit from the altar with wide grins, dancing to a song I've probably heard on Christian radio this week about God fulfilling his promises at the right time.

God, I never thought to ask for love because I never believed in it until now. But if there's still time to make such requests, and if I could have my pick, it'd be sweet Pearl I'd want to walk down the aisle with.

28
♥

Pearl Davis

There is a reason I avoid wearing anything taller than two inches. These skyscraper heels might as well come with a *proceed with caution* sign for me. Forty-five minutes of standing in them has been enough. All I plan to do is to sit at the reception, so I doubt anyone will even notice if I ditch the cocktail hour to slip into my comfy sandals that are in my car. I could use the breather.

Edwin, one of the groomsmen, keeps making unwanted advances toward me. I have a feeling he thinks he's doing me a favor by showing interest. He's Kate's cousin, and there's no way she could have resisted telling him that I'm single and searching.

But no thanks. I may be single as a Pringle, but my heart isn't in the game. It's been taken hostage by Zane, and I've tried every trick in the book to move on. At this point, I'll need divine intervention to even enjoy a nice conversation with a man that isn't him. Until then, I'm doomed to be the girl with a Zane-shaped hole in her heart.

The cocktail hour is set outdoors, using the same space as the ceremony. The tall tables are decorated with white, gold, and teal tablecloths. There's a large backdrop with Kate and Duke's names for photo ops, adorned with flowers. Music fills the air as guests mingle, chatting and sipping on drinks in the pleasant, mild weather—the warmest Massachusetts can offer in April.

I make my way over to Robyn, who seems to be hitting it off with one of the groomsmen. Another casualty of wedding small talk, I can't help but feel sorry for him. It's written all over his face—that little crush he's nursing for her.

"Hey, I'm going to grab a shoe change from the car. Shoot me a text when it's almost time for the reception," I tell her.

"Didn't think you'd last in those heels. I'll ring you up," she replies with a nudge.

I shuffle awkwardly through the parking lot. Thank God Duke and Kate decided to host both the ceremony and reception at the same venue. It's a breathtaking golf course, owned by a member of our church community who generously gifted it to them. I can only imagine how much having a free venue has alleviated their wedding expenses.

The golf course itself serves as a lush green carpet, stretching out as far as the eye can see, dotted with twinkling lights. The wedding arch is draped in cascades of white fabric and intertwined with fresh florals.

"If I hadn't noticed the cocktail hour serving virgin drinks, I'd be suspicious," Zane's voice rings out, instantly recognizable to my heart.

My heart leaps as I turn to find the most attractive man in a navy suit, crisp white shirt, and a teal tie—Zane. His hair is neatly trimmed, and my heart warms just at the sight of him. If only it wouldn't complicate things, I'd give anything to run straight to his arms. Every fiber of my being aches with how much I've missed him.

Tears threaten to spill at the overwhelming rush of emotions his presence brings.

"Zane, what are you doing here?" I manage to choke out, my voice sounding more robotic than I intended.

"Duke invited me. I couldn't miss seeing you in that dress for sure," he replies, flashing me a slow smile that sends heat creeping up my entire face.

Oh no, the dress that shows off all my insecurities.

"Pearl, you look beautiful," he says, as if he could read the doubts swirling in my mind. Despite my resolve to not seek validation from a man, his compliment somehow manages to silence the chorus of negative thoughts that plague me.

"Well, if only I knew how to walk in these heels, I wouldn't be totally embarrassed right now," I reply, trying to deflect the attention away from my self-consciousness.

"I don't know why women go through that trouble." He rubs the back of his neck in that familiar gesture.

How I've missed every little thing about him.

"That makes two of us." I feel a rush of warmth as he closes the distance between us.

He extends his arm for me to hook, and I accept without hesitation. Being near him feels reassuring, and it's not just because of my wobbly heels. There's a gut feeling that tells me letting him closer in my life could feel just as comforting.

As we stroll toward my car, we take a moment to catch up on the events of the past few weeks. I briefly share a heartwarming update about a client who has recently found a forever home with a wonderful family.

"But how do you get children that have been through hell on earth to actually share what's happened to them?" Zane asks. "I could never open up to anyone for the longest time. I'd think most kids who never received love would be that way too."

We reach my car and I pause to reflect on my sessions. "You know, children are just like us." I lean against my car, facing him. "They crave the same thing we do: to be heard, truly heard, not always being told what to do or what to think, although that also has its place in child rearing. So, my approach with them is all about listening. When they open up, even just a crack, I make sure to echo back their words. It lets them know that, one, I'm following, and, two, this is important to me instead of taking the opportunity and making it about me and what I think. And when they've said all they want to share, we unpack it together, and I add a little bit more clarity to their thoughts from being more mature and having life experience, and of course, faith. None of my sessions go without a mention of the Creator who created us as emotional beings."

He gazes at me with a smile that lights up his eyes. "You speak about your job with such passion. You really love what you do."

"I truly do. It's more than just a job to me; it's a calling, a purpose. It's a gift, being able to pay forward the kindness and guidance I received. My old therapist was like a beacon of hope, Christ-like in her compassion. If I can offer even a fraction of that to the children I work with, it would mean everything. In this fractured world, people need safe spaces filled with hope."

"Yeah, you mentioned her," he recalls, stirring memories of our late-night phone conversations. I miss those calls every night. "It's just hard to imagine you as the rebellious teenager you describe yourself as."

"The transformative power of grace," I muse, thinking back on the darkest time of my life. "Some of the families I lived with back then wouldn't recognize the person I am today. All thanks to Jesus."

He looks like he's on the verge of saying something, and for the first time, I sense admiration, almost like he could understand or even relate to the impact of Jesus in my life. There's none of his usual perplexed look or exasperated sighs.

As I swap my shoes, I try to study him, and suddenly, out of nowhere, his face breaks into laughter.

"Those have got to be the smallest feet I've seen in a while."

"Don't you dare bully me," I playfully scold, jabbing a finger in his direction. "You're more than eight inches taller than me."

I quickly straighten up, using my dress to conceal my sandals.

"No, seriously, your feet are adorable. I bet they could fit in my palm. What size are you?"

I nudge him in the side and I'm met with the unexpected firmness of his rock-solid abs. My mouth mimes a "Wow" that he probably notices.

"I'm a size six. It's not too small," I say, feeling my cheeks and ears warm with embarrassment.

Thankfully, my phone rings with Robyn's call. She tells me that they're about to head to the reception venue.

"Robyn says it's time for us to take our seats at the reception. Are you joining us? Or were you planning on heading home?"

"I wouldn't dream of going anywhere." He smirks. "I think you might need some protection looking like that. Those groomsmen might just try to steal you away."

"Oh?" I raise an eyebrow. "And why would that be a problem? I'm a single woman, after all. I should be mingling."

I know flirting with Zane always leads to the same conclusion—I end up proving to myself once again just how much I like him. Yet I let him lock eyes with me, and despite the inner warning bells, I can't resist the pull of his ocean-blue gaze.

"You want to mingle out there?" he asks, his voice carrying a hint of possessiveness and tension that wasn't there before. I notice the subtle tightening of his jaw, his body tensing up involuntarily, as if the mere thought of me mingling with someone else is causing him physical pain.

"You have a problem with that?" I ask, unable to suppress a small grin, though I reign in the squeal that wants out. I've never seen him more attractive. Jealous Zane, well, where have you been all my life?

He grabs my hand, sending shocks through my entire body as he inches closer in the empty parking lot. The sun is setting and it's casting the perfect shadow across his face, and when he opens his mouth, I feel his minty breath tingle down my neck as he gazes at me intently. "What about me? You never wanted to mingle with me," he murmurs, his eyes full of desire.

A small gasp escapes my lips. Is Zane going to kiss me here and now? And if he is, am I going to let him? Everything in me wants to bridge the gap between us, but up to this point, I've regretted all the guys I've ever kissed. I definitely don't want Zane to be another name on that list of regrets. I'm also completely done engaging in meaningless kisses and fleeting moments of passion. My future husband deserves more self-control than this. Kissing Zane would be far from forgettable; it would be a memory etched into my heart forever. I've never felt this way about anyone before.

I yank myself out of the trance he put me in and say, "I'm a bridesmaid. I can't be late." With determination in my steps, I start walking up toward the reception venue. He tries to catch up, but not in the way of someone eager to accompany me. Maybe he felt it too, that electric tension between us.

Something was about to happen. Why didn't he just go for it? Why did he give me time to think and then chicken out?

No, it's not chickening out. It's being realistic. I'm preventing another heartache.

I try to console myself with that thought, even as I can't shake the curiosity of what it would have been like to kiss Zane.

29

Zane Ortiz

Pearl doesn't hate me. In fact, it's quite the opposite. I could sense it in the way her pulse quickened under my touch on her wrist and the way her breath caught in anticipation. The moment lingered, and I could tell she wanted the kiss as much as I did. If she had wanted to reject me, she would have done so swiftly. The expectant look she gave me is all that's consuming my mind right now.

As I watch her dance with one of the groomsmen on the dance floor, she looks like she'd rather be anywhere but in his arms.

"You know, you could just go and ask her to dance," Coach says, nudging me with a grin. I'm sitting with him and his family, as the only people I know here are in the bridal party—everyone else seems to be a rabid fan.

"I don't know what you're talking about," I reply, shifting my eyes to glance at the couple on the dance floor. How could he tell who I was looking at? Duke cradles Kate's head, and they both look like they're in their own world.

"If I was blind, I probably wouldn't be your coach." He chuckles softly. "But seriously, get your behind out there and ask her to dance. She's clearly suffering with that young man."

"What makes you think she won't suffer through dancing with me?" I ask, attempting to mask my growing nerves. I haven't yet confided my interest in Pearl to anyone except Tyler and Carson, and they wouldn't have spilled the beans to Coach.

"I think she's behind the new Ortiz we've been seeing for the past two weeks," Coach remarks, his hand rubbing his freshly trimmed chin.

"Of course. She sent me to a counselor, and it's been really helpful," I dully respond, bringing the glass of lemonade to my lips. I've met with Dr. Lawson a few times, and we've also had some sessions over the phone. While we haven't made significant strides yet, he's been instrumental in guiding me through the stress of the season's end. I've talked to him a bit about my journey, and during one session, I shared that I had accepted Jesus Christ. He seemed genuinely pleased to hear about it.

"I think she did more than that. You know it too." He gives me a knowing look, indicating he's not joking. It's a side of Coach I've never seen before. Why would he suddenly be interested in my dating life?

Then it hits me—Pearl is like his daughter. By sending me out there, he's giving me his blessing to pursue her.

I smooth down my pants and rise up, feeling a bit self-conscious since I usually try to keep a low profile in large gatherings. This isn't something I'd usually do, but then again, Pearl has a way of making me do things I'd never do in another context. And it's not like I haven't been photographed since I arrived—every flash seems to catch me—but I've been avoiding direct eye contact with any camera, pretending not to notice. Even the wedding photographer seems to favor our side of the guests.

But now, all eyes will be on me as I approach Pearl. Whether she accepts my invitation to dance or sends me back to my seat is bound to make some headlines. But for Sweet P, I'm willing to take the risk.

As Pearl and her dance partner look like they're about to step away, I seize the moment, stepping up from behind her and gently reaching out my hand. "I think I'll take it from here," I say softly, catching Pearl off guard. She turns, a hint of surprise flickering in her eyes. But the guy easily lets go, he doesn't even flinch; instead, he simply nods and seems content to return to his seat.

I slip my hand onto Pearl's waist, gently turning her to face me. "What do you think you're doing?" she asks, trying hard to sound annoyed.

"What does it look like? I'm dancing with you."

"But..."

"But what? You said you came here to mingle. Let's do that." Despite my invitation, her feet remain rooted to the spot.

"Is everything a competition to you?" she asks, lifting her brow.

"Sweet P, don't pretend you were having a blast with what's-his-name over there." A huff escapes my lips as I nod toward the guy she was dancing with.

"Edwin," she blurts out, pretending to be upset with the most adorable pout.

"With Edwin," I repeat, "I've been watching you two since he asked you to dance. He was boring you to death."

"I think Kate asked him to keep me company, so he has duty written all over his face and moves." She winces.

"Well, Coach only asked me to ask you for a dance because I couldn't take my eyes off you," I say, with a little bow and extending my hand to her once more. Perhaps she didn't appreciate the surprise of me grabbing her hand without consent. While some women may swoon at the *command* to dance with me, Pearl might be different. She deserves to be treated like royalty if she so wishes. So, with all the flair I can muster, I add, "Would you do me the great honor of gracing me with this dance, my sweet Pearl?"

When she blushes and offers a shy smile, I pull her closer to me, and we sway slowly to the rhythm of the song. Every point of contact between us sends a jolt of electricity through me, and I can feel my heart racing with each gentle movement.

Our pace synchronizes, each movement tentative yet perfectly coordinated. With each sway, we draw closer, the space between us diminishing until I feel Pearl's shoulder relaxing against me. Our dance evolves into a wordless conversation.

She finally allows her head to rest on my chest.

There's something here.

There's a connection between us, an electric current that crackles in the air, and I need to know if Pearl feels it too.

Throughout the second song, we share fleeting glances. Pearl's rainforest eyes are practically sparkling with this new intensity.

She's never allowed our eyes to search each other's depths for this long. I catch a glimpse of a vulnerability she's fully concealed beneath layers of distance and avoidance.

I never dared to hope for this—despite the unanswered calls, the ignored texts, the distance—but Pearl has been hiding her feelings for me.

Why? All I've done is show her that I'm interested in her.

Did she doubt it? Does she not know I would literally move mountains for her?

Pearl lifts her head, tucking her chin into the hollow of my chest, I instinctively lower mine to meet hers, aiming to gently tip our foreheads together.

But she suddenly halts, saying, "I need some air."

I desperately hope this is her way of signaling that our first kiss shouldn't happen in public and end up in a headline. There's probably a camera lurking somewhere, waiting to capture this moment.

I follow her, matching her steps, but she turns and looks surprised, "You need air too?"

I realize my assumption was wishful thinking.

"I'm not letting you out of my sight looking like that."

She frowns and keeps walking.

We get to the patio adjacent to where the ceremony took place, a spacious area overlooking the golf course that could easily accommodate an outdoor reception. The gentle glow of low lights bathes the surroundings, while the distant sounds of children playing outside remind me of my childhood aversion to weddings—being forced to sit with Dad was always a punishment. Above us, the moon hangs in the sky, adorned with a sprinkling of stars.

"Men can be so superficial," Pearl scoffs, her words accompanied by an array of animated gestures. "So this dress I'm never gonna wear again is making you follow me all night. And this heavy makeup. Is that why you're looking at me like that? This isn't my real face, you know."

Despite her dramatic gestures, I know she knows this isn't why I'm here. Why does she keep fighting this? Fighting us?

"Unless you've forgotten, you once called me a stalker, and you've already warned me about the way I looked at you at their engagement party," I counter, pointing toward the reception hall where Kate and Duke are now dancing with their parents. "And I'm pretty sure you weren't wearing this dress and had less noticeable makeup then."

She turns her face away, remaining silent.

I remove my jacket and approach her, gently placing it over her shoulders. The day began with warmth, but now a gentle breeze stirs, and her sleeveless dress, while stunning, leaves her vulnerable to the chill. I want to admire her, but not at the cost of her comfort. Normally, Pearl carries a cardigan or sweater, but today, she's without one, much like at the engagement party.

She looks at me and mouths a "thank you," without making a sound.

"Listen, I think you're beautiful. Like, out-of-this-world kind of beautiful," I say, my heart thudding, hoping she hears my sincerity. "The very first time I laid my eyes on you, it was as if time itself paused, just like in those Hollywood movies, and everyone else in that coffee shop blurred."

I reach out for her hand, our fingers intertwining effortlessly. "But that's not all. You are kind, you are extremely caring, you live out your faith in the way you care about people. You're a joy to be around, and you have this amazing way of really listening to me without any hint of judgment."

"You really think all that about me?" she asks, her eyes searching mine.

"And so much more, Sweet P," I reply, now trailing my fingers over her arms as I pull her closer.

"I have to confess something. I never *just* wanted to be friends with you."

She giggles and playfully rolls her eyes.

What a beauty!

"Now that I've come clean, would you let me kiss you?"

Hesitation flickers across her face, and when she shakes her head, a sharp pain shoots through my chest. But then, with a barely audible voice, she whispers a shy *yes*, sending a rush of relief flooding over me. I almost want to double-check if that's really what she means because in my world, shaking your head signals "no." But there's no time for overthinking when her eyes are shining like puppy-dog's and her eyelashes are fluttering shut.

I gently cradle her head and lean in to claim her lips in a kiss that feels like it could last a lifetime. She doesn't wait to mirror back all the emotions I've been feeling. They're strong, intense, and I can tell Pearl isn't holding back. She hasn't said it with words yet, but it feels like she's claiming me too.

I have to pull back. Not because I want this moment to end, but because we can't kiss as if we're already something more when she hasn't even expressed her feelings. Maybe she hasn't even told herself the truth.

I need to tell her how I feel, that four-letter word I've never uttered to anyone before. I hope it doesn't scare her away but rather encourages her to open up as well.

"Pearl, I—" I start, but she interrupts me.

"I don't think this was a good idea," she breathlessly says.

"What wasn't a good idea? Me kissing you, or you kissing me back with the same fervor?" If not more, if I do say so myself.

I had to hold the fort for both of us, to not get carried away in what I now know would be dangerous territory. Oh, right, I still need to tell her my testimony. One thing at a time. She needs to admit she has feelings for me.

"I made a mistake. I didn't mean to lead you on. We can't be together." Her voice is trembling and her eyes are brimming with tears. She puts a hand on her mouth and rushes back inside—with my jacket.

Losing the jacket is nothing compared to the pain I feel in my chest.

I stay rooted to the spot where she left me, gazing up at the sky. I raise both hands, intertwining my fingers behind my head. Where does one go from here?

I've fallen for a woman who considers her feelings for me a mistake.

Ouch, that stings.

30

Zane Ortiz

After the "mistake" with Pearl, I made my way back to the reception hall to inform Coach and his family that I was heading home. Even though part of me wanted to slip away unnoticed, I couldn't bring myself to do so. Before he let me go, he shared with me that there's an important announcement he wants to make after practice, just before the press release. He asked me to spread the word to everyone.

I'm not sure why he specifically singled me out for this task. Usually, it's Tyler who's the go-to guy for these kinds of things—he knows how to keep tabs on everyone.

Maybe Coach has noticed how I've been stepping up my game lately—handling conflicts, putting in the extra effort in practice, and improving my teamwork off the ice.

Perhaps the potential he once saw in me wasn't just wishful thinking after all.

I send out a quick text, reminding everyone to dust off their professional attire and brace themselves for an announcement from Coach and the board.

My gut tells me it's about Tyler's retirement, a fact everyone's already clued in on. I know the media's itching to know what's next for the team.

If those old rumors turn out to be true, and Coach has truly managed to convince the board to overlook my past suspensions, tomorrow could change everything for me.

It's just tough to get hyped up for it all after what happened with Pearl.

I need to apologize, even if there's a chance she won't reply. If by some strange twist of fate, I completely misunderstood our moment, I can only hope she'll forgive me. But apologizing for what could easily be classified as the best kiss of my life? That definitely doesn't feel normal to me.

Zane

> I'm sorry if I forced you into something you didn't want. I tried my best to respect you, your body, and the boundaries I believe you hold. But you running away made me realize I still failed you somehow. It won't happen again.

Her text bubble appears and I sit up straight on my bed. It's been a while since I saw her *typing*. It feels like we're texting for the first time—a giddy feeling rushes over me.

Sweet P

> You didn't do anything wrong, Zane. Sorry for running away with your jacket.

Zane

> Keep the jacket, my clothes always look better on you. But why did you really run away? That kiss... It felt like you were finally showing me what's really in your heart.

Sweet P

> The heart is deceitful. Just because we had a moment that felt right to both of us doesn't mean it was a good idea in the grand scheme of things.

Zane

> So you agree it felt right? Can I call you? I have something I wanted to share with you today.

Sweet P

> I know tonight brought a lot of confusion, and really, it's all my fault. I've known your intentions since the very first day, and I owe you a big apology. Can we talk another time?

> Zane
>
> Let me know when you're ready to talk. Good night.

Frustration tightens my fingers into fists. I'm not one to give up without a fight, but Pearl leaves me no choice. She looks like she's already made up her mind that we won't work, and there isn't much I can do about that if she doesn't want to at least tell me why.

I say a half-hearted prayer before sinking into my sheets. I need to get some adequate hours of sleep tonight—tomorrow could be a big day.

·♥·♥·♥·♥·♥·

If I'd known that accepting Jesus would lead me to this moment, would I have rushed into it?

My pride and ego resist, but there's a nudge telling me I need to talk to him. I stride over to where Trent is, the clang of metal against metal echoing as players prepare their gear, the scent of sweat and equipment spray filling the air.

Everything about this moment feels routine, yet what I'm about to say is a first.

"Trent, can we talk?" I ask, my voice muffled by the loud conversations around us.

He glances over, his red eyebrows arching in annoyance. "You can't wait for it to be official before you start gloating?"

"What are you talking about?"

"Stop pretending like you aren't here to talk about captaincy. We all know that's what the meeting and press release is about."

"That's not why I want to talk to you. Whether Coach announces me as the new captain or not, I'd like to turn over a new leaf with you."

Trent's ginger eyebrows shoot up again, and I can see the skepticism in his eyes. This isn't something I'd normally volunteer for, especially because all the conflicts we've had were instigated by him, but I'm convinced I need to do it. "I've been hoping to be a better teammate, on and off the ice. We've had our differences, but nothing that should keep us at odds or affect our ability to work together." I pause to let my words sink in. His forehead muscles relax slightly as my words seem to resonate. "I apologize for everything. I hope we can focus on being a team from now on."

Trent gives me a strained smile and reaches out to shake my extended hand. I nod, turning on my heel, and head back to my stall.

"That was something," Carson says, swaying his head.

"I don't know what got into me, but it needed to be done. I've been tired of these petty fights for a while now."

"Call it the Holy Spirit." Carson shrugs.

"I'm not sure what he thought of that though. He gave me a weird look."

"*'So far as it depends on you, live peaceably with all.'* Romans 12:18," Tyler spits out a verse.

"Do you always have one of those ready to serve?" I jab him from behind.

"You'd be surprised how much of the Bible you retain if you make it a priority to read it every day. And with my kids, we memorize verses together. It's become a big part of my life."

"I struggle with reading. I doubt that'll ever be like me."

"There are so many options nowadays," Carson adds. "You can listen to the audio version if that's what you'd prefer. I do that when I'm working out."

"I like that idea. I'll give it a try."

Coach enters our locker rooms to check on us. "Is everyone set?" he asks, standing tall in the doorway.

I look around and see everyone nodding. "Yes, sir," we all respond in unison, looking sharp.

We file into the hallway and head to a meeting room where the board is waiting for us.

Coach takes his place at the front while we settle into the seats arranged in a round conference-room style.

"Thank you all for a remarkable season. This has truly been one of our best," Coach begins, setting the tone for the meeting.

Glancing around, I catch Tyler's smirk in my direction. The other guys seem focused, hanging on every word the coach says.

"With Tyler retiring at the end of the season," I turn my attention back to Coach, knowing this is the moment, "we've selected a new captain to lead the Glaciers forward."

Anticipation sweeps through the room. Coach continues, emphasizing the significant role the new captain will undertake, filling Tyler's skates.

"Ortiz," Coach's voice breaks through the tension, drawing all eyes to the front where he sits, his gaze fixed on me. "It is with great pride that I announce you as the new captain of the Glaciers. Your hard work, commitment, teamwork on and off the ice, and recent improvements in your chemistry with the team have demonstrated your dedication."

Excitement, and a touch of nervousness surge through me. It's official—I've been chosen to fill Tyler's shoes.

What an honor!

Everyone applauds, including Trent, though his expression remains stoic, but maybe that's just his face. After all, I need to get to know the guy better outside of our tiffs.

"Tyler." Coach turns to our retiring captain. "Thank you for your years of dedication and leadership. Your legacy is woven into this team's fabric."

Tyler nods, pride and nostalgia flickering in his eyes. I can easily tell he'll miss being on the team but he's chosen his family—a man with his priorities in the right order.

Coach moves on to brief us about the press release. There will be many questions for me, but the first person I want to share this big news with is the one who thinks kissing me was a mistake.

31
♥

Pearl Davis

"Did you pray about it? What is the Holy Spirit nudging you to do?" Beatrice asks gently. Despite the patchy connection, I know what great lengths she has gone so that I can hear her voice. When I emailed her about feeling lost and needing a mentor's opinion, she immediately responded with reassurance. She promised to make the trek into the city just to have this conversation with me. Unfortunately, Fynn had to stay back in the village to teach Sunday School. With a 12-hour time difference, it was already Sunday in Cambodia while it was late Saturday night for me.

"I've been asking God to remove Zane from my life since the first time I met him. I knew he'd be trouble for my heart. I knew it then, and yet, I still let him get closer. Now, I feel like God is punishing me for not going with my first instinct."

"Have you considered that your restlessness may be stemming from not seeking God's will in this matter? It seems to me that you told Him what you wanted and never took the time to listen. But prayer is not just about asking the Lord for what we want. It's about presenting our requests and asking for His will to be done in our lives."

"But he's an unbeliever!" I say, my words tinged with a hint of pride. I quickly attempt to soften my tone, adding, "God's word makes it clear whom we should and shouldn't be yoked with."

"You've already mentioned that honey, but from what you've recounted, Zane doesn't seem to be leading you away from God. It makes me wonder if you could be the light in *his* life. I don't mean that you need to jump into a romantic relationship with him, but you and Robyn can invite him to be part of your church family. You just need to make things clear to him." Suddenly, a light bulb switches on in my mind.

He's attended our church. He's allowed me to share my faith in our conversations without pushing me away. He even mentioned that one of the things he admires about me is how I live out my faith by loving others.

And that kiss had so much self-control and restraint, and it definitely wasn't my doing.

I hadn't delved past "we kissed at the wedding" with Beatrice. She didn't need to know all the details of the best kiss of my life.

"I'm afraid to get hurt again, Beatrice. Clay asked me to be a light in his life, but it turned out to just be an excuse to get into bed with me. By the time I realized his true intentions, my heart was already fully invested. I'd rather die than go through that again with Zane."

Tears fill the corner of my eyes. Thinking the best of people has caused more damage to my heart than good. And although every fiber of my being tells me that Zane is different, I'm still too afraid. The thought of him hurting me is my biggest fear. I've never felt this way about anyone before, and I'm certain the pain would surpass all the heartbreaks I've endured if he were to break my heart.

"Don't say that. The guys you've dated in the past pursued you for the wrong reasons, and I admire how cautious you've become. It shows you've learned. But now, fear seems to be guiding all your decisions. And why haven't you told Zane all this? Keeping him at arm's length without giving him a valid reason is probably why he keeps coming back," she urges in her motherly tone.

I sink onto my bed to lie on my back, prop the phone on my pillow and put it on speaker. My gaze drifts up at the ceiling as I voice my fears, "I fear that if I explain to him that the only reason I can't date him is because I can't be with someone who doesn't share my faith in Jesus, he might just claim he does to win me over. Just like he attended church at the drop of a hat."

"Once again, acting out of fear isn't the same as exercising caution. After Clay, you have more discernment now. Remember, you can always ask the Lord to help you discern his true intentions."

I rub my eyes, feeling more confused than ever. All I wanted out of this conversation was clarity, but even Beatrice isn't helping, much like Robyn.

Who will?

"Honey, remember, God is never without a plan. Trust Him in every aspect of your life and that includes your love life. Release the grip of past hurts and your preconceived ideas of how love should find you. Your wisdom is admirable, but relying solely on it won't suffice if you're seeking to honor your Savior.

"Coming to Jesus with humility for guidance might seem daunting, but remember, your future isn't a mystery to Him. While you may believe you're guarding your heart, God's care for you surpasses your own understanding. Trust Him. The Holy Spirit will never mislead you. Whether it's parting ways with Zane or letting him into your life, peace will accompany the path God leads you on, even if you have to make a hard decision."

She concludes with a prayer for me and hangs up, leaving me to ponder her words.

The hardest part of all this is that Beatrice is spot-on. I haven't once prayed for God's will. I've only asked and begged for Zane to vanish from my heart and life. And despite my efforts to distance myself from him, the peace I've been chasing still eludes me.

I close my eyes, still lying on my back, and whisper softly, "Jesus, I realize now that I've been approaching You with my own plans, driven by fear rather than faith. I haven't sought Your will for my relationship with Zane. Today, I surrender control to You. Show me clearly whether Zane should remain in my life or not. I want to trust You with my heart and not rely solely on my past experiences, though I acknowledge they've served their purpose. Lord, lead me where You will."

In my prayer, something became clear. After Clay, I stopped trusting the Lord in matters of my heart. He was the first relationship where I felt peace because I wasn't constantly trying to compromise my values as I had in past relationships.

His genuine interest in knowing the Lord reassured me, and I was happy to be part of *his testimony*. My dream of getting married way before thirty was on the verge of becoming a reality. So when he shattered my heart, I was left utterly bewildered.

Why hadn't God intervened? Why had He even allowed me to meet Clay? All I wanted was a Christ-centered relationship, so it didn't make sense that I had been deceived. And now, with Zane, I've been fighting my own battle rather than allowing God to shield me because I doubted whether He could prevent a heartbreak, since He hadn't in the past.

May the trials in my life draw me closer to Jesus, not drive me further away. Help me to fully trust you again, Lord.

I hear a thud at my door, and Robyn bursts in. She sees the tears on my face and wraps her arms around me. "Don't worry, I'm not sad. Beatrice gave me some food for thought."

"Great. I came to show you this," she says, holding her phone up to my face, displaying Zane's social media profile.

"What? I don't think I need to see his pictures to remind myself of him," I scoff. If she thinks I haven't already stalked his profile since the wedding, she really overestimates me.

"Read the bio, P," she insists, her voice pitched with excitement.

I reluctantly glance at the screen and read aloud, "2 Corinthians 5:17." A rush of warmth fills my insides as I recite the verse silently to myself.

'Therefore, if anyone is in Christ, he is a new creation. The old has passed away; behold, the new has come'

It's one of my favorite verses.

"Did he tell you anything about this?" Robyn asks, her eyes wide.

"No, nothing. I mean, I haven't exactly given him the chance to tell me anything, but this...has he always had this in his bio?" I'm now sitting up.

"Negative. I don't check his profile often because he rarely posts anything, but the last time I looked, it was just his team and position on there."

"I just prayed for clarity about him. It's the first time I've truly asked for God's will in this situation."

"Well, consider this your sign. Next time I need prayers answered quickly, I'll know who to turn to!" She tosses her hair.

Biting my lip, I say, "But this could also mean nothing. Lots of people walk around with verses tattooed on their bodies and they aren't devoted Christians. Maybe he thought it was a nice verse. I've shared many verses with him before, and he's never asked me to stop."

"If this were a verse from the book of Proverbs, Psalms, or even Ecclesiastes, I'd be tempted to follow that train of thought," she holds my gaze, "but, P, let's be honest, that doesn't sound like a verse anyone would willy-nilly put on their bio. Especially not someone like Zane who admitted to not believing in God over a month ago."

"You're right. I just hate tooting my own horn for nothing. But I must admit, I'm intrigued."

"I think you should talk to him. Not just about reliving that magical kiss, but also to find out what he's been up to these past few weeks."

I shove a pillow in her face.

After the wedding, I told Robyn how I felt like Cinderella when Zane kissed me. I still picture his crestfallen expression when I referred to it as a mistake, and it breaks my heart. It didn't feel wrong, but labeling it as such made avoiding him and his out-of-this-world charm seem easier.

"You know all about hockey. Do you think hockey players who bump into other people all day can really want salvation? Especially someone as popular as Zane?"

"Pearl!" Now she's the one who hits me hard with the pillow. "You know Jesus came to save everyone. Anyone who calls on His name will be saved. And Zane Ortiz? I can easily picture him as a devoted Christian," she says, closing her eyes as if having faith has a certain look. "In fact, he's super close to the team's captain, Tyler Collymore, who is unashamedly Christian. And I think Carson Adler is a believer too."

It always surprises me how she still refers to them by their first and last names, especially since she's already met Zane.

"I know. I sound awful. I just really don't want to get my hopes up. I'll text him," I say, picking up my phone. It's too late, he probably won't see it until tomorrow.

"All right. We need to get some sleep if we're planning to make it to the baptism tomorrow," Robyn says, rising from my bed. I almost forgot about tomorrow.

Robyn and I like to attend every baptism. Some people come without their families to celebrate, and the church invites anyone who wants to join in welcoming their new life with them. Baptism Sunday is my favorite. It always reminds me of how my life changed when I sank into that water and rose back up. That's when the verse in Zane's bio became a truth in my life.

"Right. Good night, Robs. Love you." I blow her a kiss.

"Love you too, P. I'm rooting for you two," she says, holding up two fingers like a peace sign, slightly tilted for effect.

"Of course you are," I reply with a grin as she closes the door.

If I thought sleep was hard to come by this week, the possibility of Zane accepting Jesus in his life isn't going to let me catch a wink.

32

Zane Ortiz

Staring at the raindrops trickling down the window, each one seems to have a purpose, a path to follow. They glide like they're gracefully washing away my doubts and uncertainties. The loud thunder rolls and the intensifying flashes of lightning are adding to the moment. A flutter in my chest accompanies a faint voice telling me my life is about to change, and not just because Pearl texted me. In just a few minutes, I'll be immersed in water that symbolizes leaving behind my old life and stepping into a new life with Jesus.

I'm getting baptized.

A small group of people—men, women, and even a couple of teenagers—gather in the stuffy classroom of the church. We've been meeting for an hour in the evenings this week to learn about baptism, and it's incredible to see how the same God who has been working in my life has also been active in the lives of so many others. Each person here has experienced different struggles and has recognized their need for Him.

Some days this week, I questioned whether I truly wanted to make this public declaration of following Christ. I feared that I might falter or make mistakes, and worried about being judged for every little choice I make moving forward. But what I feared even more was that the same God who led me to make amends with Trent last week might continue to ask me to do even harder things—things I strongly oppose, like reconciling with Dad.

Aunt Melissa called again this week, urging me to visit, but I made it clear that I won't come if Dad is still around.

I badly want to believe that God won't ask me to forgive him, considering all he's put me through and how dangerous being close to him can be. But if there's anything I've learned in the past three weeks about God, it's that He is a God of many chances. It would be consistent with His character to extend His mercy to my father too.

I shake my head and glance at the pastor once more. I know any hesitation I'm feeling is not from the Lord. Maybe if I take this act of faith and step into the water, God will remove my dad from my life for another decade of peace.

The pastor, with a cheerful tone, asks, "Any questions about anything before we say a prayer and head over to get baptized?"

A teenage boy, likely between fourteen and sixteen, speaks up. "Is it still safe if I can't swim?"

This prompts laughter from the others.

Regaining composure, the pastor reassures him, "Don, it's a tank. You won't be drowning, and I'll be right there holding you the whole time."

A woman in her thirties then asks, "Can my husband take pictures?"

"Of course," he responds warmly. "This is a day you'll want to remember for the rest of your life. Having some visuals to look back on will be a gift."

He pauses briefly, scanning the group for any more questions. "All right, if there aren't any more questions, let's give thanks to the Lord."

The pastor then leads us in a prayer, "Gracious Heavenly Father, thank You for bringing each person gathered here to this momentous occasion. We pray for courage and faith for those stepping into the water today, knowing that You are with them every step of the way. We pray against any fears or doubts that may linger in their hearts. Grant them peace and assurance, not only for today but also as they journey through this life, by the grace of our Lord Jesus Christ. Amen."

We make a beeline for the hallway, and a few people who haven't changed into their baptism clothes go do so in the restrooms. I'm glad I came wearing shorts and a basic t-shirt, and left my church clothes in the car.

I appreciate that the baptism is happening before the main service, away from the gaze of everyone. I didn't want this moment to be publicized or shared widely—I wanted to keep it intimate and personal. The only person I wish I had told is Pearl. If only I had known last night that she would text me past midnight, I would have asked her to come to church an hour earlier. She'd have loved it.

Hopefully, I'll have the chance to sit with her during the service and share the news.

After a burly man with intricate tattoos covering his arms takes his turn, I step forward to enter the water next.

The feeling in my heart is indescribable. It's more than just excitement; there's a deep sense of anticipation. I can't quite put into words what I think will happen, but I strongly sense that something significant is about to unfold—and it feels like a good thing, like an answer to my prayers.

I ascend the stairs and step into the baptismal tank. The water rises to my waistline as the pastor firmly holds onto me, guiding me through the process. He instructs me to cross my hands over my chest and hold my nose.

"Have you accepted Jesus as your personal savior?" he asks. When I respond affirmatively, he grasps my arm and declares, "Because of your faith in Jesus and in obedience to His command, I baptize you, Zane Ortiz, in the name of the Father, and of the Son, and of the Holy Spirit."

With that, he lowers me backward into the water until my whole body is immersed, then immediately raises me up. As I emerge from the water, shaking my head a bit to clear my wet hair from my face. I take in a deep breath, my chest expanding as my lungs fill with air once more.

When I open my eyes, the first person I see in complete bewilderment is Pearl—my Sweet P.

My heart swells in my chest, and I offer a quick prayer of thanksgiving before stepping out of the water. Most people have their families here, and I didn't even bother to ask Tyler or Carson to attend. Yet Pearl is here early for the service for whatever reason, and I have her as a witness. Actually, two witnesses, because Robyn is standing next to her.

Pearl comes running to me, and before she falls into my arms, I give her a look that says, "I'm wet." She ignores my warning and squeezes me tightly around my middle. I still can't believe this is real.

"Zane, are my eyes deceiving me or did you just get baptized?"

I pull out of the embrace to see her face. She looks as beautiful as ever, wearing an olive green overall dress with her hair styled in a high ponytail, two curled strands framing her face. She accessorized with gold earrings and a necklace. Her fruity fragrance is more noticeable than usual.

"I've been tuning in to the online sermons using the link you shared with me, and about three weeks ago, I accepted Christ into my life. Then this week, I decided to join the baptism class." My words tumble out, a smile spreading across my face to match hers.

She opens her mouth, but no words come out.

"I was about to tell you at the wedding before—," I start, but she interrupts.

"Zane, I'm so sorry for the way I left. You don't deserve how I've been treating you." Her eyes glisten with tears, almost spilling over. "Will you find it in your heart to forgive me? I know I don't deserve your friendship anymore."

Her words echo the conversation that brought me here today. I didn't deserve God's forgiveness and love, yet here I am, baptized and embraced by the family of Christians.

"I'm not going to pretend that hearing you call our kiss a mistake didn't hurt." I scratch the back of my neck. "But what matters is that you texted me and you're here. I'm sorry I haven't replied. I had a baptism to get to." I chuckle.

"A baptism, huh. I definitely need the entire story."

"I need to go clean up before I get hypothermia. Can I take you out on a date after church? I'll tell you everything."

"Of course," she says, hugging me again as if she forgot I was still soaked. "I'll go congratulate the others. That's why Robyn and I come. We never miss Baptism Sunday."

I give her a full smile.

She's absolutely the one for me.

· ♥ · ♥ · ♥ · ♥ · ♥ ·

"What's surprising is how the word didn't manage to get out. Our church is pretty small, and keeping secrets isn't our forte," Pearl remarks as we wait to be seated at an Italian restaurant we discovered we both like.

The rain has stopped, and outside, the April flowers are abloom with a kaleidoscope of colors, each petal a reminder of the changing season. Spring is here, and with it comes my first date with Pearl.

"Pastor made sure to emphasize keeping my privacy. He didn't want the news to spread and draw unexpected crowds. If the media had caught wind of my baptism, they would have shown up too."

A tall waitress, almost my height, approaches us and after recognizing me, she apologizes for the wait. I usually don't wait in lines because I order everything online, but I don't mind standing as long as needed if I'm with Pearl.

I pull out a chair for Pearl, inviting her to sit. She gracefully accepts and takes her seat. After settling into my own chair, I extend my hand across our small table, and she places her small hand in mine.

"I know this is our first date, but I really want to have many more. Can you let me officially pursue you?" I ask locking my gaze with hers.

She nods, her lips pursed as if she's holding back words.

"That's a yes, right?" I clarify, recalling how last time she shook her head but said yes with her words.

"It's a yes, Zane. I'd love it if you pursued me."

"Is it because I got baptized today? You should have told me that's all I needed to do to finally get you to go out with me."

She playfully pushes my hand away. "Please don't tell me you did that for me."

I throw my head back laughing. "I was just kidding. No, I accepted Jesus into my life a few weeks ago. It all started when you invited me to church though. I couldn't get the pastor's message out of my head."

"Pastor Marcus," she adds.

"Yes, sorry about that, Pastor Marcus. I keep forgetting he has a name. When he taught, I realized I didn't really know much about Jesus' life beyond the part where he died for our sins. Even that had never been well explained to me. His sermon challenged everything I had lived for and believed in. I had so many questions, and it turns out Jesus isn't afraid of my questions. One of my friends and teammates, who is a Christian, helped me through the roadblocks I was facing. It was like he had an answer for everything I doubted, and when he didn't, he would encourage me to pray about it and read the Bible. Slowly, everything I thought I stood for melted away in the overwhelming knowledge that God sent His son to die for someone like me. It's all been a whirlwind."

My eyes dart around, unable to hold her intense gaze. I muster all my strength to resist the urge to cup her face and pull her into my arms.

"I've never been happier for a testimony in my life," she says, wiping away a tear.

I reach out and gently hold her cheek. "You should be. If I hadn't met you and been so enamored with you from the start, I don't know how much longer it would have taken for me to find *the* way."

She takes my hand and brings it to her mouth, softly kissing it. Her lips are as tender as they were at the wedding, and all too suddenly, all the fears I had about what my life following Christ would look like melt away.

33

Pearl Davis

"So, Captain, huh?" I muse as Zane and I leisurely walk through the park after an amazing lunch, where he shared with me how the Lord revealed Himself to him.

The sun on my neck rivals the thunderstorm that welcomed Robyn and me this morning. The air carries the sweet scent of blossoming flowers, mixed with the earthy scent of recent rain. Vibrant tulips and daffodils add splashes of pink, yellow, and orange to the landscape, their petals dancing in the soft breeze.

Families are spread out across the park, relishing picnics on checkered blankets, while children's laughter fill the air and dogs frolic in the grass.

This date feels like something out of a perfect picture.

There have been countless moments in my life when God answered prayers in ways that surpassed my understanding. This is one of those moments. I have no doubt that Zane is the *one* for me. It may have taken me a while to realize it, but I wouldn't change a single thing about how

God brought us together. Knowing that my role in his faith journey is minimal reassures me that *this* is genuine.

"Yes, I still can't wrap my head around it, and I probably should have seen it coming. Tyler is a great captain, and I have big skates to fill."

"Skates?" I ask, noticing the use of "skates" instead of "shoes." He grins in response. "Why weren't Tyler and Carson here? Did you tell them you were getting baptized?"

"No, actually, I didn't think to invite anyone. I didn't realize people usually invite friends and family. I'm so glad you showed up. At least you and Robyn were there to witness it."

"You should tell them now. They'll be so excited. I can't imagine a friend of mine getting baptized and me not knowing about it."

"I will, but first let me get used to this," he says, glancing down at our intertwined fingers. "I never thought holding hands could feel this way."

"How does it feel?" I ask, meeting his gaze as he takes my other hand.

"It feels like I never want to let you go, my Sweet P," he confesses, drawing me in with his eyes. "It's like your hands were always meant to be in mine." He steps closer. "It feels right, it feels real, and it feels promising."

All I manage to say before our faces meet in a kiss is, "I feel all that too." The kiss is just as magical as the first one, and my heart is content to have no doubts about Zane and me. We deepen the kiss, but all too soon, he pulls away.

"Are you going to keep doing that?" I ask dryly.

"I have to stop before I lose all sense. And with you kissing me so passionately, one of us needs to make sure we're staying in the safe zone." His words melt my insides.

"It feels so good to be on the other side of this conversation. I'm used to being the boundary police in my relationships, and honestly, it was exhausting and never worked out well. I desperately needed someone who could take charge."

"Well, I'm only a man and just human. Please don't overestimate me." He gently holds my chin, causing tingles to spread through my face and neck. "But I really want to do this right. You are worth the wait." He gives me a peck on the nose, and I feel a lump forming in my throat as I struggle to hold back the tears that come with finally hearing those genuine words from a man.

"I won't overestimate you, but I want you to know that I trust you." The words slip out.

I don't even have to try. It's like I naturally trust him.

"It means so much to hear you say this, Sweet P. I'm sorry if I reminded you so much of your ex," he says, his brow furrowed. I use my thumb to smooth it out. Earlier at lunch, I told him about Clay and the real reason I kept pushing him away.

"It wasn't anything you did. I realized I had stopped relying on God in my love life because He didn't prevent men from hurting me in the past. Just by looking at you, I concluded you might be like the others and did what I thought was best for me and my relationship with Jesus—I ghosted you.

"But yesterday, I was reminded that in this fallen world, people hurt each other, and painful circumstances happen and will keep on happening. Despite this, God remains good and true all the time. Trusting Him doesn't mean understanding everything, but standing by Him even when we don't understand our circumstances."

He gently tugs my hand, gesturing for me to sit on the bench, and I follow him. "Being a devoted Christian is hard."

I pull my eyebrows together in a frown, not because I believe that carrying your cross daily is a walk in the park—although moments like sitting here with Zane in this beautiful park are erasing all the hardships I've been through from my memory—but he talks about it like there's a specific challenge he's referring to. "What makes you say that?"

"My dad's out and he wants to see me."

My eyes widen and my mouth falls open.

"I keep having this unsettling feeling that God will make me go see him. And I just don't think he deserves for me to hear him out. That would be like giving him another chance to hurt me. Look at me, it's taken twenty-eight years for me to finally see life differently. I can't let him ruin this next chapter of my life."

"Zane, the Lord never forces us to do anything. That would go against the free will He gave us," I say gently, opening his palm and intertwining our fingers. "But I also just told you that fear of being hurt again caused me to not give you a chance before, and look at how well we fit." We both glance down at our joined hands. "Don't let fear be the lens through which you view your life anymore. I learned this lesson yesterday."

"It's not the same thing. I've never done anything to hurt you. But my dad..." He pauses, his expression troubled. "He's bad news. And the worst part is that my aunt believes he's changed. I know it's only a matter of time before she calls me telling me about some new damage he's caused."

I lock eyes with him. "Forgiving is a huge part of the Christian life, and trust me, I know it's hard. But when He asks you to give your dad another chance—when, not if—He will give you the strength to do so."

"How will I know for sure that he's asking me to do it and it's not just misplaced pity?"

"The same way you knew you needed to accept Him into your heart and get baptized soon after." Memories of all the times Jesus made things clear to me and led me to act on them, despite my emotions, come to mind. "And the peace that will accompany that decision will be another sign."

"I'm afraid it's already happening. This was my biggest fear before getting baptized, and after today's sermon, I've had this lingering, strong feeling about it. Pastor Marcus didn't even mention anything close to forgiveness," he says, clenching his teeth, the tension visible in his jaw.

I wrap my arms around his broad shoulders. "I promise you, everything will be okay. I'm here for you as much as you need me."

He kisses my cheek. "I feel like I'm dreaming. Are we really together?"

I bat my eyes, allowing myself to be drawn into the ocean of his gaze. "Well, you haven't exactly called me your girlfriend yet, and you just said that the strong feeling you had since our church service wasn't about me but about your dad." I try hard to keep a serious face. "So, you tell me." I unwrap my arms and fold them against my chest. "Are we *really* together?"

"I'm sorry, Sweet P. I've never been on a date with a woman I loved. I'm not sure what the protocol is."

A gasp escapes my lips.

"See, I can't even wait for the right moment before confessing my true feelings. But, Pearl Davis, I'm in love with you, and I have been for a long time now. You're my girlfriend now."

Words leave my brain and my heart races at the speed of light.

All I want to do is to say it back.

He puts a finger on my lips. "You don't have to say it back. I want you to feel the same confidence I feel about us when you do."

He seals my mouth with a kiss, one that I'm sure is meant to stop me from saying it back. And that's okay, because I want it to be special when he hears it.

34

Zane Ortiz

"What if this is a mistake?" I turn to Pearl, her head resting on my shoulder as the plane touches down in Chicago.

"It's a huge leap of faith, but it's not a mistake," she reassures me, gently squeezing my hand.

When the plane begins to settle, passengers start to rise, and we watch as everyone hurriedly retrieves their bags from the overhead compartments.

Choosing to reroute my trip to Chicago instead of Detroit is the reason I'm flying commercial with Pearl. But being with her in economy feels far richer than any luxury charter flight could offer.

Pearl makes a move to grab her carry-on, but I beat her to it. With a grin, I gather both mine and hers, along with the business suit I brought along, and hand her my light backpack.

Outside the cramped aircraft, she hooks her arm in mine.

O'Hare Airport is one of the biggest and busiest airports I've ever been to. I like the architecture and the efficient TSA, but the chaos is too much. Pearl and I try to weave through as fast as we can.

The delicious scent of food wafts from nearby eateries, enticing us since it's already two in the afternoon and we still haven't had lunch. The snacks Pearl packed for us have long vanished from my system. But as tempting as the smells are, we resist the urge to indulge. Aunt Melissa begged to cook us a late lunch, and showing up with anything less than a voracious appetite would definitely hurt her feelings.

It's been a week since Pearl and I started dating, and every day I discover something new about her. Whether it's stories from her childhood or insights into her work—though she never calls it that. It's her calling and ministry—I'm still awestruck by her being mine.

She's more than just an amazing girlfriend—she's become my best friend, my rock, and my biggest cheerleader. If it weren't for her encouragement, I doubt I would have listened to the little voice in my heart that has, for so long, urged me to see Dad. I could have easily kept brushing it off, delaying the inevitable, but Pearl's unwavering belief in me made me believe I could do it.

Even now, as we stand at the rental service, about to pick up a car and drive fifteen minutes to see the man I'd long ago written off, I still feel the pull to turn around and head straight to Detroit, where our final game awaits in just a couple of days. But Pearl and I have made plans to make

THE GAME SHE HATES

the drive tomorrow. We aligned our arrival with the rest of the team.

Everything feels so right between Pearl and me, but there's one thing she hasn't said yet: those three life-changing words, "I love you." It's not that I've been dwelling on it every time I've said it, expecting her to echo it back. Her actions speak volumes—the way she looks at me, the way she devotes all her time to us, the kisses she doesn't hold back—it's as if I already have her whole heart.

But there's a nagging fear in the back of my mind. Her not saying it back leaves a tiny crack in our otherwise perfect connection. We've promised each other honesty and open communication, but I don't want to jeopardize anything by bringing it up too soon. It's only been a week, and she hasn't given me any reason to doubt her commitment.

Maybe I'll give it another week before I broach the subject. I'll need to find the right words, though. I don't want her to feel pressured or rushed into saying something she's not ready to express. It's just that her actions already say it all, and I can't shake this feeling that she's holding back for a specific reason.

Maybe after I talk to my dad, she'll see how serious I am about obeying God, and she'll fully trust me to eventually lead her when we get married someday. Yes, she hasn't said she loves me yet, but she's made enough allusions to our future together to give me hope.

So you see why I'm a little worried.

We settle into the rental car and begin our drive to Aunt Melissa's house, my heart quickens its pace, much like it has the entire flight here.

The sun shines brightly. It's a perfect summer day. I grew up in Chicago, but I never miss living in the city. It was a bit much, especially with all the memories of my childhood.

Life in Bedford has been kind to me, and it's not a long drive from Boston when I need a little chaos—which usually comes from the team anyway.

"I don't even know what to say to him."

"Listen," Pearl says gently, her voice calming my nerves. "Don't try to come up with the perfect words. Just give him a chance to tell you what he's called you for, and trust the Holy Spirit to guide your conversation."

"But what if I lash out? After all these years of resentment, I don't trust myself to speak kindly to him."

She reaches out and her touch immediately grounds me. She offers a prayer for self-control and wisdom and asks God to glorify himself today. When she finishes, her hand gives mine a gentle squeeze.

I turn to her for a split second, offering a smile, before returning my attention to the road.

She is wearing a cozy baby blue sweater, yoga pants, and sandals, her hair swept up in a messy bun. I'm always attracted to her, but when she goes to the Father for me, that attraction is almost uncontainable.

It's usually expected for a man to make a woman feel protected and safe, but she also does that for me in ways I never knew I needed. I feel secure, grounded and at peace with her because she involves Jesus in every aspect of her life—and now mine too.

We pull into Aunt Melissa's driveway, and memories of past summers spent here come flooding back. This was always my sanctuary, my escape from Dad's torment. Now he's inside, and I'm going in.

Can I really do this?

"Look at me," Pearl commands, and I quickly turn to meet her gaze, wondering if she can see the hesitation written all over my face.

I don't want to disappoint her.

"I need you to know something important before you go in there." She releases a long, slow breath. "I love you with every fiber of my being, every beat of my heart, and every breath that graces my lips. I can't express enough how amazing you are as a person. Even if you don't feel ready and choose not to go in there, my love for you is irrevocable. My heart belongs to you, Zane Ortiz, no matter what you choose to do right now."

Moisture invades my eyes. "I really needed to hear you say this. I'm having second thoughts, but there's a deep feeling that's convinced I need to go."

"I won't leave your side unless you tell me to."

"I won't ask you to go anywhere. And you're used to working through family dynamics, so I could use you in every capacity," I quip.

She swats my arm. "Zane, I'm *not* your therapist and never have been. I'm your girlfriend who *loves* you."

"I love you too, Sweet P." I pull her hands and kiss her knuckles.

"I love you even more," Pearl says with a bubbly voice. I suppose now we can compete to see who loves the other one more. It used to seem like a silly game, but now it's all I want to do. Though we don't have time for that, I have a feeling either Aunt Melissa or Dad already knows we're here.

When the door opens, I realize I've been holding my breath, and I exhale in relief when I see Aunt Melissa.

"Honey!" she exclaims, pulling me into a tight hug that lingers. "I've missed you so much. And look at you!" She steps back to take a good look at me, her hands gently patting my arms. "You've become even more handsome."

Then she notices Pearl behind me and almost knocks me out of the way. "And you must be Pearl Davis!" Aunt Melissa envelops Pearl in a hug. "I've heard so much about you, darling. Pictures don't do you justice—you are a thousand times prettier in person."

I'd only sent one selfie of us to Aunt Melissa because Pearl and I weren't the best at taking pictures together. The photos that circulated of us were from Kate and Duke's wedding, where we danced together, and others were from coffee shops where people caught glimpses of us. According to Pearl, they didn't always capture her best angles. Maybe she's right, if Aunt Melissa thinks she's prettier in person.

In my opinion, nothing could dim Pearl's beauty. Not even a bad picture.

"Thank you, Mrs...," Pearl says, realizing I never told her Aunt Melissa's last name.

Aunt Melissa quickly interrupts. "Please call me Mel. Everyone does. I'd love it even more if you called me Aunt Mel, like this one here." She points to me.

"No problem, Aunt Mel. I don't have a lot of family, and I'd never pass up such an opportunity," Pearl replies easily.

"Well, the pleasure is mine. I never had kids, and I'm too much for Zane, so we're a perfect match." Aunt Mel chuckles as she leads Pearl inside.

We step into the living room that smells exactly like I remember—spicy notes of cinnamon and nutmeg. I immediately see Dad sitting in the living room on the love seat near the entranceway.

Surprisingly, the feeling I have when I see him isn't what I expected. There's no rage, no anger brewing up inside me, no churning in my stomach. Instead, my heart feels expanded in my chest, and a gulp in my throat struggles to find release. I feel a small hand in mine, reminding me to breathe and not succumb to this strange emotion.

When I step on the carpet to take a seat, he remains seated and doesn't stand to greet me. I'm glad because I can't recall how I ever greeted him when I was young.

As a teenager, I didn't even bother acknowledging his presence in a room. But when I was a kid, I held onto the hope that things would improve if I showed him how well-behaved and perfect I could be. I tried so hard back then, thinking he would eventually like me.

We all sit down, and Aunt Melissa asks if we want anything to drink. My hunger and thirst are barely registering—I can't name anything—but Pearl asks a Sprite for me and a water for herself.

She knows me so well.

And she loves me.

Whatever happens in this living room isn't going to ruin the day the love of my life told me she loves me too.

"You look good, Zane. Thanks for coming," Dad says.

And he looks good too. Prison time has definitely made him look sober and in the best shape I've ever seen him in. But I say nothing. How can I compliment the man? I'm not angry like I thought, but I'm also not happy to be here.

"I'm just going to go ahead and say what I've been waiting to tell you for the past decade. And if your girlfriend—"

"Pearl, and she's staying here with me," I interrupt.

"Yeah, I was going to say if Pearl wants to be here for it, she's welcome to," he finishes the sentence in his rumbling voice.

"I've spent every day of these ten years reflecting on the man I was, on the father I failed to be. Being locked away forced me to confront the demons that led me to ruin your childhood and damage your life.

"I want you to know that the man who walked into that prison cell is not the same man standing before you now, and not because I've done lots of soul-searching and I decided to change my ways, but because Jesus Christ entered my life.

"I don't expect you to forgive me like He did. I didn't deserve His forgiveness, and I don't deserve yours either. I know apologies alone aren't enough. They can't erase the pain or make up for lost time. But I want you to know that I am sorry. If I could go back..." A tear rolls down his cheek. "If I could go back, I'd change the perspective I had before you were born."

"You knew you were going to be an awful dad even before I was born?" I manage to ask.

"Yes," he mumbles, looking down. "When Alice was pregnant and having all sorts of health issues, they told her there was a risk she wouldn't make it if she went through with the pregnancy. They wanted to try to save her but that meant losing you, and she would have none of it. She was resolute in her faith in God, thinking He could save both of you. Even if her prayers went unanswered, she was determined to see you through." Tears started streaming down his face. "I resented you before you even arrived because of those agonizing months she endured. When the unthinkable occurred and she passed while you survived, my deepest fear became a harsh reality I faced every day by simply looking at you." He covered his face with his hand, not wiping the tears but trying to hide how much it still hurts.

"Really, it wasn't you that I was mad at. I was mad at everyone else—Alice's determination, the doctors who couldn't save her, and the God she placed her trust in. It's no excuse, but alcohol became my refuge, the only thing that dulled the pain, and I clung to it faithfully."

My heart feels like it's exploding into a million pieces with this new information no one cared to give me before. My mom knew she probably wasn't going to live?

Like Dad, I can't comprehend her logic. Why did she think being motherless was better than not being born at all?

A thought that distinctly isn't mine emerges in my mind, drawing a parallel with Jesus. He died for us so we may live. And that's what my mom did. She gave me this life—a life that, though bitter in the beginning, has led me to the woman holding my hand, bravely fighting back tears to be strong for me.

Now, I can live this life with the assurance of salvation and the hope of seeing Mom in the next life.

For the first time, my eyes see Dad differently—not just as the source of my pain, but as someone who carried his own burdens. Despite his bad choices, I realize his suffering was genuine.

Something in me tells me Mom would love it very much if I stood up and wrapped my arms around Dad and told him I forgave him, and so I did.

35

Pearl Davis

Perched on the edge of my seat, I wrap my arms around myself in a futile attempt to ward off the freezing air of the Detroit arena. I'm grateful for Zane's jersey layered on top of my red dress, but I should have also brought a scarf for my cold legs.

I can't tear my eyes away from Zane, tracing his every move as he zooms across the ice. Every flick of his stick, every shot he takes, and every bend of his legs fills me with a flutter of concern. It's like I'm out there with him, feeling every slip and stumble as if it were my own.

When things start to get dicey, I'm closing my eyes and praying for his safety, hoping he stays steady on his skates.

I'm still getting used to the attention that comes with being known as Zane's girl. There have been enough headlines about us that people are recognizing me from every angle. That's why I tried to look my best today, I simply never know when a fan might snap a picture.

In the beginning, I couldn't shake off the insecurity that crept in when I compared myself to his exes, who seem to be straight out of a magazine. But I've been working on letting go of those joy-stealing comparisons. I might not fit the mold of what social media deems as beautiful, but Zane sees me as his perfect match, and the way he treasures me is all that matters to me. He's the man I prayed for, and he exceeds all my expectations abundantly every single day.

Zane's dad and aunt are sitting with me. The four of us drove together in Zane's rental car to Detroit from Chicago. While Zane and his dad were trying to bridge the gap to find a connection, Aunt Melissa and I instantly hit it off over our shared love of books. We discovered we had the same taste in genres and had devoured the works of the same authors. So, naturally, the entire drive was spent gushing over our favorite reads and swapping recommendations.

She is an incredible woman of faith, with a maternal aura that enveloped me. Even though she didn't have kids of her own, she cared for Zane like he was hers.

Her eyes sparkled with love whenever she spoke of her late husband, and her positivity was truly inspiring. Curious about her ability to discuss him without succumbing to tears, I asked her secret. She explained that she faced each day with hope, knowing she was one day closer to reuniting with him and Jesus' sustenance is all she needs to make it through.

I loved being around her, and I could see myself and Zane spending many of our holidays with her and his dad. It also didn't hurt that she was a hugger like me.

Behind us, Tyler's wife, Lacey and her four kids cheer enthusiastically. When the referee's orange armband goes up for an icing call, Tyler's wife leans over to explain. "The other team shot the puck behind that red line in the center," she says, pointing to it. "So they have to stop the play and do a face-off." She's been our go-to for all things hockey, and her adorable children have chimed in with their own explanations a few times.

Aunt Melissa chuckles, admitting, "I've never had much luck following the puck. But then again, I'm not really trying." She pauses, then adds with a grin, "I only watch his games to catch glimpses of my boy when I miss him."

Ditto. My focus hasn't left Zane either but when anyone on his team scores, I'm cheering with the enthusiasm of someone who understands the game inside out.

Unlike Aunt Melissa, who's been to Zane's games in Chicago a few times, Zane's dad is experiencing it all for the first time, taking in every moment with wide-eyed wonder. He's the most focused of us all. He seems to be following all the action on the ice and his lack of questions suggests he understands the proceedings better than us.

With striking blue eyes and the same hair color as his son, he's a mirror image of Zane in many ways.

When Zane is substituted off the ice, he sends a smirk in our direction and winks at me. My cheeks flush with warmth, and I respond by miming, "I love you." To my delight, he is able to read my lips and places his hand over his chest in the shape of a heart. Even behind his helmet, his happiness is off the chart.

During the last timeout, I give Robyn a call. Even though I know she's not missing the game, a twinge of guilt tugs at me for being here while she's not. "Hey, Robs."

"P, we're totally crushing it!" she screams excitedly over the phone. "I can't even wrap my head around the fact that you're at the final game. Oh, and thanks a bunch for the pictures. I've already posted them on my socials. If people want to think I'm chilling in VIP seats in Detroit instead of being on our cozy couch at home, well, that's on them."

I let out a chuckle. "I can't believe I'm here either. But I do feel bad. Why didn't you take Zane up on the offer for a flight here? Turning down a hockey game, all expenses paid, doesn't sound like you at all."

"Wow, so I don't jump at the chance to take advantage of your boyfriend for once, and you feel bad?"

"You know Zane loves treating you to a game. It's not taking advantage if he offers."

"I'm kidding. I promised Charlie I'd help her find a place to stay. She's being evicted from her apartment. And turns out, she likes hockey too. So she came by and we're watching the game together."

"Hmm, where's my best friend and what have you done with her?" I joke. Robyn was your typical introvert. Making friends never came easy to her, but ever since meeting Charlie on baptism Sunday, they've stayed in touch. It actually makes me feel less guilty for spending so much time with Zane, knowing Robyn isn't hanging out by herself. But still, it's pretty intriguing. I'm curious to see the girl

Robyn's tolerating, on top of me. I already know I'm quite a handful for her.

"I'm not kidding. I'm really looking forward to you meeting her. I have a feeling you two will hit it off. She's a bit younger than us, around four years or so, but she's the sweetest person. Honestly, she reminds me a lot of you."

"Ah, now it all makes sense. I'm glad you've found a friend and it's kind of cool knowing I have some influence over your choices. *Hehe*."

"Don't flatter yourself too much," she teases. "The game is back on. Here's hoping Zane hits the ice again. We could really use another one of his goals."

"I know I still have my cheering voice ready to root for him. Anyways, love you! Say hi to Charlie for me. We'll definitely hang out when I come back."

The call ends, and right on cue, Zane strides back onto the ice, looking ready to finish strong.

· ♥ · ♥ · ♥ · ♥ · ♥ ·

Zane emerges from the locker room, looking all cleaned up. I'm standing near the door where he asked me to wait for him, surrounded by Tyler's family and a few other spouses and girlfriends. We're both traveling back with his team tomorrow afternoon, but his dad and aunt had to leave immediately after the game because they have an early flight in the morning.

As soon as he spots me, he rushes over and envelops me in a hug that seems to swallow me whole. He lifts me effortlessly, as if I weigh no more than a leaf, my legs dangling in the air. I relish how perfectly I fit inside his arms, as if there's a cocoon of space just meant for me. His scent, a blend of citrus and spice from his body wash, wafts into my senses, making me want to cling to him forever.

He is dressed in sweatpants and a cozy Glaciers hoodie and guides me to settle by the now nearly deserted rink, where the echoes of the game still linger.

"This wasn't like the semi-finals; it was intense, lots of pushing and shoving," I say, still in awe of how well he played. The Glaciers emerged victorious with a 4-2 score, and Zane was credited with two goals. Fans were screaming his name, and it was clear he had maintained his reputation as one of the best, yet fame never went to his head. Fans will never know how genuinely good of a person he is on top of playing so well.

"Ah, that's the championship for you—the grand finale of the season. Everyone's brought out their A-game, and the rivalry with the opposing team today runs deep. They used to dominate until we broke their winning streak, so they were giving it their all." His eyes are still alight with the intensity of the game.

"You were incredible out there. I loved every moment you were on the ice."

"Thanks. Having my dad and Aunt Mel at the game was special. I never imagined he'd ever see me play. And every time I looked at you...I felt invincible. Your presence fuels me in ways I can't even describe." He locks his gaze with mine, and like always, his eyes captivate me entirely but I don't ever have to fight it anymore.

"Then I'll never miss any of your games ever again, Captain," I promise, a wide grin spreading across my face as I envision myself cheering him on from the stands at every game. The crowd had erupted in wild roars at the announcement of Zane replacing Tyler as captain next season.

"So, does this mean you no longer hate this game?" Zane asks, pointing to the ice.

"Ladies and gentlemen, presenting your newest hockey fanatic!" I announce with a flourish, giving myself a round of applause and earning a bemused look from Zane.

"As long as the new fanatic only wears my jersey," he adds with a lopsided grin.

"Always 12." I raise my hand as if taking an oath.

With a gentle, calloused touch, Zane cups my cheeks, his warmth spreading through me. We close our eyes, and our lips meet in a tender and deep kiss. A surge of passion, previously withheld, surprises me, and he whispers against my lips, "That's me telling you I love you, in case you missed hearing it."

"I love you too, Zane Ortiz," I murmur, my heart overflowing with love.

36

Epilogue

The jungle-themed murals of monkeys swinging from trees, ducks and elephants in a river, birds perched on branches, and a lion reigning as king of the scene are coming together beautifully on the teal-painted walls that Pearl is putting the finishing touches on. I crane my neck to admire her progress and gauge how she's feeling.

"Did I mention today how incredibly proud I am of you?" I ask, watching her work with admiration. She has been a huge help with decorating the nursery and has done a fantastic job.

"Only about ten times," she replies with a wide grin, though her expression quickly changes when another contraction hits. The discomfort seems to be intensifying with each passing hour.

"I'm sorry, love. Why don't we head to the hospital and see how everything's going?" I reach out gently to help her up.

"If you keep apologizing after every contraction, my love, you have a long day—and maybe night—ahead of you," she says with a half-smile. Each time a contraction grips her, her expression sours, and she holds her breath, as though something is prodding her until she releases it. It's difficult for me to witness her in that state.

"And no, I don't want to go to the hospital too early. That's a common mindset for first-time moms. I want to let labor progress naturally at home."

She had explained to me multiple times that hospitals and stressful environments can sometimes slow down the progress of labor. However, as I watch her become increasingly uncomfortable throughout the day, I find myself struggling to support her decision to wait it out at home.

Neither of us have experienced this before, and throughout the entire pregnancy, I've battled relentless anxiety over the possibility of something terrible happening to her. Without Jesus, these past nine months would have been plagued with nightly panic attacks, haunted by the darkest fears of losing my sweet wife, similar to how my dad lost my mom.

I was still working on memorizing my Bible verses, but there was a song that really helped me with Psalm 34:4: *'I sought the Lord, and he answered me and delivered me from all my fears.'*

It was a comforting reminder that fear isn't from God and that only He can deliver me from it. Pearl also loved reassuring me with this whenever I struggled.

"Okay, but will you tell me if things get out of hand?" I ask, searching her eyes.

"I promise." Her voice is steady as she looks into my eyes, her hand gently resting on her rounded belly like she wasn't in major pain just a few minutes ago. I walk toward her, squat to press a kiss to her forehead, my hand caressing the gentle curve that now cradles a new life—a life created by God, the fruit of our love.

I knew marrying the love of my life soon after saying "I love you" was the craziest and best decision I ever made. But I hadn't anticipated the abundance of blessings that have poured down on us since we exchanged vows.

All I know for certain is that I don't deserve this life, yet I believe that God hasn't withheld any good thing from us, including the heartache that has made expecting our rainbow baby even sweeter and miraculous.

"Help me up?" she asks. "I want to send the finished product to Charlie and Robs."

Instead of simply offering her my arm and making her do the work of getting up, I hold both of her arms and lift her. As she stands up, there's a sudden splashing sound, and fluid begins to trickle down her leg.

"We're going to be parents!" she shouts, seemingly unfazed by the gush of water.

I'm thrown into confusion, my mind racing as I try to recall our labor checklist. "Okay, where is my labor list again?" I mutter, frantically digging my phone out of my pocket. "Let me grab the bags, start the car to warm it, and get you inside. Well, not necessarily in that order—I'll start the car first!" I blurt out, my voice betraying my escalating panic. My hands shake as I fumble with the keys.

THE GAME SHE HATES

"Relax," Pearl replies calmly, her feet still planted on the ground. "Everyone at church told me first labors can be pretty long, so the baby probably won't be here for a while. Let me freshen up, change clothes, and then we can head to the hospital."

"Okay, freshening up sounds good. Do you need any help?" I ask, trying to embody the calm I had hoped to maintain on this day.

"No, you can warm up the car and text Dad, Aunt Mel, and the girls. I'll be quick."

·♥ · ♥ · ♥ · ♥ · ♥·

"Buddy, I got something for you," I say softly, cradling the smallest human I've ever seen in my arms and bringing him to my lap. I turn his sleeping face to the first gift I want him to have—the tiniest pair of skates. "You're going to love hockey."

I glance over at Pearl, who looks beyond exhausted, a little lifeless even, but at the same time, her eyes sparkle with joy like never before. It's been seven hours since her water broke, and after what felt like an Olympic marathon, Micah is finally here. I thought I knew thrill from hockey, but today surpasses anything I've ever experienced.

Suddenly, the room bursts open. Aunt Melissa, Dad, Robyn, and Charlie all enter, having waited outside anxiously. They gush over Micah and comment on how he's a mini-me. The split second we saw the color of his eyes immediately after birth revealed they aren't forest green like Pearl's—they are light blue.

"Can we *now* know his name?" Robyn asks eagerly, taking the baby from Aunt Melissa. Pearl insisted on keeping the name between us until someone guessed it, and no one ever did.

"This is Micah Xavier Ortiz," Pearl announces proudly.

"You named him after me?" Dad beams.

I chose his middle name.

"Yes, I want him to feel connected to his grandpa." I pat his shoulder.

Dad has truly changed. Even after forgiving him, I still had doubts about his ability to stay on the right path. However, during the two years he's been out of jail, he showed a remarkable transformation. He has truly surrendered his life to Jesus Christ and his change gradually patched the wounds in my heart, one by one.

"Sweet P, how does it feel to have your own flesh and blood?" I ask, turning to my sweet wife. Her eyes are fixed on Micah, as if she's still processing the transition from having him all to herself in her womb to now sharing him with all of us.

"I feel like God's favorite right now. I married a handsome, godly man, and now I have a baby that looks exactly like him. I've never been happier," she replies, her voice tired yet accompanied by a serene smile.

Her words compel me to fall to my knees in humble gratitude to God.

Thank you Jesus they both made it.

The End

Thank you

Thank you so much for giving *The Game She Hates* a chance. If it brought you joy, I'd be honored if you could take a moment to leave a review. It can be as short as one sentence that describes how you feel about Zane and Pearl. As an indie author, your reviews help others discover this book, and your support means everything!

The Game She Hates marks my debut into Christian romance. While all my books were written with a Christian worldview, answering God's call to write stories that clearly point to Jesus didn't come without its fears and doubts. Yet, inspired by the incredible Christian fiction community, I took a leap of faith.

The journey to God's will is often full of obstacles, but with His guidance, I was able to find my way.

Many people were part of this journey—my alpha and beta readers, you deserve all the praise for the makeover you gave this story.

My editor, it was so nice to work with someone who shares the same faith.

My bestie turned social media manager, you have no idea how much you've simplified my life.

My parents and brothers, you've always been beyond supportive.

Special thanks to David for making my beautiful cover. I am a blessed sister to have you in my corner.

And lastly to my husband who plays with our energetic toddler while I write these stories, I am blessed beyond measure to call you mine.

instagram.com/ella_marie_author

facebook.com/profile.php?id=61556613820971

tiktok.com/@ella_marie_author?_t=8jxp5d6kiar&_r=1

goodreads.com/author/show/48055375.Ella_Marie

bookbub.com/profile/ella-marie

amazon.com/stores/Ella-Marie/author/B0CB1T1MT2

Also by Ella Marie

My Clean and Sweet Romance Collection
Eyes For My Grumpy Billionaire Boss
Eyes For My Brother's Best Friend
Eyes For My Worst Neighbor
Eyes For My Off-Limits Crush
My FREE Novella
My Best Friend Next Door

About the author

Ella Marie is a pen name of a wife to the man of her dreams, and a mama to a cute little boy. Jesus is her Lord and personal Savior, guiding her in all aspects of life. After publishing her first clean and sweet romance series, God put it on her heart to share the greatest gift in her life—Jesus—in her love stories.

All her future books will not only be heart-melting but will also point readers toward the love and grace of Jesus Christ. Expect to see broken characters finding healing, faith, hope, and of course, love in each of her Christ-centered love stories.

Her greatest prayer is that her books will encourage readers to live out their faith boldly, deepen their relationship with Jesus, and remember that no other book is to be cherished like God's letter to us— the Bible.

Join Ella Marie's Book Besties private group on Facebook

Printed in Great Britain
by Amazon